ALLEN

P9-AFS-014

3 1833 05555 8511

"Are we going to talk about the kiss?"

Even though she knew they were alone, she glanced around the room. "No."

"Why not?"

"I'm not interested in talking about it."

"What if I am?"

She gave him a flat stare, trying to dismiss the sensation prickling her skin. "Fine," she said tightly. "Let's talk. There's more between us than chemistry or attraction or—"

"Lust," he suggested.

Her stomach dipped. "Whatever you want to call it, there's something else."

"Like what?" Wariness tightened his features.

She was going for it. She wanted answers and he had them. "Like the fact that you screwed up my life and I want to know why."

ROMANCE

MAR 0 5 2010

Dear Reader,

Since I began THE HOT ZONE series, I've had frequent requests to write books for the two friends of the heroine of book one, *Burning Love*. *The Private Bodyguard* (Jan 2010) was the story of Dr. Meredith Boren and fire investigator Gage Parrish. In this last book, Detective Robin Daly gets her turn with fire marshal Nate Houston in *The Forbidden Bride*.

Five years ago, Robin was left at the altar. Nate not only witnessed the most humiliating day of her life, he caused it by persuading her fiancé to call off their wedding. Her ex refused to explain why he jilted her, and not knowing has eaten at Robin for years.

She thought—hoped!—she'd seen the last of Nate, but he's back, heading up a task force investigating a series of arson-murders that she's been assigned to. Forced to work with the man responsible for harpooning her wedding, Robin must find the killer without killing Nate in the process.

I've thoroughly enjoyed writing this series. Thank you for taking the journey with me.

Best wishes,

Debra Cowan

DEBRA
COWAN

The Forbidden Bride

Silhouette®
Romantic
SUSPENSE

If you purchased this book without a cover you should be aware that this book is stolen property. It was reported as "unsold and destroyed" to the publisher, and neither the author nor the publisher has received any payment for this "stripped book."

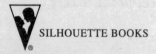

SILHOUETTE BOOKS

ISBN-13: 978-0-373-27672-1

Recycling programs
for this product may
not exist in your area.

THE FORBIDDEN BRIDE

Copyright © 2010 by Debra S. Cowan

All rights reserved. Except for use in any review, the reproduction or utilization of this work in whole or in part in any form by any electronic, mechanical or other means, now known or hereafter invented, including xerography, photocopying and recording, or in any information storage or retrieval system, is forbidden without the written permission of the editorial office, Silhouette Books, 233 Broadway, New York, NY 10279 U.S.A.

This is a work of fiction. Names, characters, places and incidents are either the product of the author's imagination or are used fictitiously, and any resemblance to actual persons, living or dead, business establishments, events or locales is entirely coincidental.

This edition published by arrangement with Harlequin Books S.A.

For questions and comments about the quality of this book please contact us at Customer_eCare@Harlequin.ca.

® and TM are trademarks of Harlequin Books S.A., used under license. Trademarks indicated with ® are registered in the United States Patent and Trademark Office, the Canadian Trade Marks Office and in other countries.

Visit Silhouette Books at www.eHarlequin.com

Printed in U.S.A.

Books by Debra Cowan

DEBRA COWAN

Like many writers, Debra made up stories in her head as a child. Her B.A. in English was obtained with the intention of following family tradition and becoming a schoolteacher, but after she wrote her first novel, there was no looking back. After years of working another job in addition to writing, she now devotes herself full-time to penning both historical and contemporary romances. An avid history buff, Debra enjoys traveling. She has visited places as diverse as Europe and Honduras, where she and her husband served as part of a medical mission team. Born in the foothills of the Kiamichi Mountains, Debra still lives in her native Oklahoma with her husband and their two beagles, Maggie and Domino.

Debra invites her readers to contact her at P.O. Box 30123, Coffee Creek Station, Edmond, OK 73003-0003 or via e-mail at her Web site, www.debracowan.net.

Acknowledgment

There were many generous people who helped with research from the beginning of this miniseries, especially the two men who never left me in the lurch. For the years they put up with this author and all her pesky questions, a million thanks to David Wiist, retired Chief of Fire Prevention, Edmond, OK, and Jack Goldhorn, PIO, Norfolk Fire Rescue, Norfolk, VA.

Chapter 1

The last time Nate Houston had been this close to Robin Daly she had been wearing a wedding dress. And the gorgeous detective wouldn't be any happier to see him now than she had five years earlier.

Just after eight on a Thursday morning, Nate parked his black SUV in a fairly new subdivision. He had taken a job with the Oklahoma State Fire Marshal's office six months earlier, but his business at this hours-old fire scene with Presley fire investigator Collier McClain wasn't official.

The June air was warm, the wind gusting occasionally. White clouds scooted across a clear blue sky. The smoke had dissipated, though its acrid odor hung thick in the air. The fire was out, the firefighters gone.

Water from the hoses puddled along the street, saturated the neatly trimmed lawns. Gouged earth and pockets of mud marked spots across neighboring yards where the firefighters had dug in and battled the flames. A single police cruiser sat at the end of the scene nearest Nate.

After showing his badge to the patrol officer guarding the scene, he pulled on a pair of steel-soled boots over his shoes, to protect his feet from sharp objects and hot spots.

Ahead, parked at the curb in front of a soot-streaked home, Nate saw a white pickup and a dark blue sedan. The pickup belonged to McClain, a longtime friend from college. The dark-haired, rangy man stood a few feet from what had been the garage, talking to a petite brunette who had her back to Nate.

Just the sight of her tightened his chest.

Procedure between Presley's police and fire departments stated that if a dead body at a fire scene was determined to be homicide and an arson, a police officer and a fire investigator worked the case together.

Neither Collier nor Robin had requested help from the state fire marshal's office. But Nate had compiled data on recent fires that made him suspect a serial fire setter was at work. If any of his information could help catch this firebug more quickly, help stop more fatalities, he had to share what he knew.

Even if it meant dealing with an armed woman who'd probably rather shoot him than look at him.

Muscles taut, Nate started across the sodden yard toward Collier and Robin. She would have caught his attention even if she hadn't been wearing that drop-dead red top. He couldn't seem to stop his gaze from skimming over her trim waist and the sleek flare of her hips in khaki slacks. Absently, he noticed the badge and holster clipped on to the waistband of her pants.

Her dark sable hair was in a neat twist low on her

nape, several silky strands feathering her neck right behind her ear. At the wedding, the satiny mass had been swept up in a style that bared the graceful line of her throat.

"I've finished the walk-around," Collier was saying. "The structure is secure, if you want to take another look—"

McClain broke off as Nate neared and a grin spread across his face. "Hey."

"Morning."

Robin turned, and when she recognized him Nate saw shock, disbelief and a fury in those blue eyes that cut through him like a cold, sharp wind.

Just like the last time he'd seen her.

Then her face went blank and her hand closed over the butt of her gun.

Even with that stay-back slant to her jaw, she was a pretty woman. The misty blue eyes and dark hair were striking with her pink-and-white rose petal skin. As he mentally mapped her full breasts and slender curves, a little current of energy zipped through him.

The purely physical reaction took him by surprise. When he had last seen Robin, he had been trying to work things out with his now-ex-wife, so he hadn't noticed much more than the fact that Daly was pretty. He noticed more than that now.

Dark brows arched delicately over thick-lashed eyes. Her skin was as pure and smooth as ivory, her mouth slicked with pale pink gloss. Clean, classic lines emphasized her high cheekbones and the soft curve of her jaw. The jaw that went tight when he reached her. He nodded. "Robin."

Her lips flattened. "Houston."

Collier looked from one to the other. "I'd introduce the two of you, but I get the feeling you've met."

"Yeah." Nate supposed she would never forgive him for what he'd done, but he would do it again in a heartbeat. Even though he had often regretted the hurt she had suffered, he hadn't doubted his decision once. Not then. Not now.

He and Collier shook hands as the other man said to Robin, "Nate recently started work at the state fire marshal's office."

"Hmm."

"How's the new house?" his friend asked.

"I'm settling in." He slid a hand into the pocket of his navy uniform pants. "It's nice to have a little land. I missed that while I lived in Chicago."

"What brings you by?" Collier asked.

Daly's laser-sharp gaze took Nate apart. It wouldn't surprise him if she drew down on him at any moment, so he got on with it. "I have some information I think you might need on your case."

"You can probably do without me for this," Robin said to Collier.

"Actually, this concerns you, too," Nate said. "Finding you here saves me a trip to the police department."

"Oh? Well, whatever I can do to help *you*."

Ouch. The silky words were a pointed reference to when he had tried to help *her*. Aware of the way McClain's eyes narrowed on both of them, Nate kept his focus squarely on the reason he'd come. "Presley's first fire-murder back in April got my attention, then about a month ago, I was assigned to investigate a fire in Warren."

"I heard about that blaze," Collier said.

There was more interest than anger in Robin's face now.

Nate continued, "When I first began my investigation, there was still a living victim, but as of last week that changed. The man who owned the restaurant that was torched died in the hospital after hanging on for almost three weeks."

"So, now you have one fire-murder and we have three, counting the husband and wife who died here last night," Robin observed coolly. "Is that the only similarity? People dying in these fires?"

"No." Nate could well imagine her turning that piercing look on a suspect. "Your first scene and mine showed signs of forced entry, either through a window or door. Both victims were bound and gagged, then burned in their beds. I bet that was the case here, too."

When he glanced at Collier, the man nodded. Nate went on, "The fire at my crime scene was started with chlorine powder in an envelope adhered to an exposed rafter with petroleum jelly."

"A signature which is unique enough to raise a red flag," Collier said. "Made with items anyone can buy."

"It can take anywhere from a few minutes to a few hours for the petroleum jelly to penetrate the envelope and ignite."

"Which gives an arsonist time to flee a scene and establish an alibi." Robin pushed away a strand of dark hair.

"Right." Nate's attention was caught by her hand and the fact that she didn't wear a wedding ring. Had she never gotten married?

Irritated that his thoughts had wandered there, he pinched the bridge of his nose. "These cases also share the same cooling-off period. The time between your first fire-murder and mine was twenty-seven days. Now, twenty-seven days after the blaze I'm investigating, you have a new fire-murder."

"You're talking about a serial arsonist," she said.

"Yes." He dragged a hand across the taut muscles of his nape.

The petite detective exchanged a look with Collier, who cursed under his breath.

"Did you eliminate suicide as a possibility?" Nate asked.

Collier nodded. "Yes, definitely."

"Same for my first victim."

"Have you taken your suspicions to Fire Marshal Burke?" Collier asked.

"Not yet, but I plan to. There's more, though. I've seen this signature before. A big case I had several years back."

"Do you have any idea who this guy is?" Robin asked brusquely. "You first encountered him in Chicago and now he's shown up here?"

Nate was surprised Daly had noticed the earlier reference to where he had lived before.

"No," he said. "It's not the same guy."

"How do you know?" she challenged.

"Because I put that SOB in prison seven years ago. And when I realized what we were dealing with, I checked on him. He's still locked up."

Collier frowned. "So, we have a copycat."

Nate hoped with everything in him that that was the case. Because, if they weren't dealing with some twisted disciple setting these fires, he had made a mistake. A dangerous and possibly career-killing one.

Robin's blue gaze met his. "Or you screwed up and put the wrong guy away."

His jaw clenched. He was tempted to categorically deny it, but that wouldn't help their investigation or his. "I don't think I did, but it's a possibility."

He hadn't thought her eyes could get any colder. Wrong. She was looking at him with the same glacial disdain that had been in her eyes five years earlier.

"If I did arrest the wrong guy, and the real torch is still out there," he said, "it is possible that he followed me from Chicago, although I doubt that, too."

Her eyes narrowed. "Was your case up there personal?"

He gave a sharp nod. "During his run of six arsons, he killed a total of twenty-two people. The last blaze was at a nursing home and eighteen of its residents died. So did three firefighters."

"I remember that. It made the national news."

"Yes." One of the firefighters killed by that bastard was Nate's father, but he saw no reason to tell her that.

"So?" Robin tilted her head. "What kind of person are we looking for?"

"Caucasian for sure, the same as all the other victims. As for more of a profile, I don't have enough information yet to determine if the firesetter is male or female."

"Before you got here," Collier said, "Robin was telling me she's found no connection between these victims and our first one."

"Not so far anyway," she put in quietly. "And no one remembers seeing anyone who seemed out of place."

"Since this accelerant takes a while to ignite," Nate observed, "someone might have seen something and not connected it with the fire."

Beneath the lingering smoke, he caught a faint whiff

of soap and woman. Her hand still covered the grip of her gun, as though she were itching to use it. On him.

Fatigue pinched her refined features. "I'll reinterview everyone I've talked to, in both our cases."

"Good idea."

"Thanks for the information, Nate," Collier said. "The more we have, the better."

"Maybe it will help catch this torch faster. I'd appreciate it if you let me know what you find here."

"No problem."

"I'll let you two get back to work then."

"Okay. See you later." Collier lifted a hand in farewell.

Robin said nothing and Nate was glad. As far as he was concerned, she'd said enough.

He started across the yard toward his SUV, her earlier words circling round in his head. *Or you screwed up.*

He hadn't, not concerning the man responsible for killing his father. Nate refused to let himself second-guess his work on that case or the conviction that followed.

Regarding these current fire-murders, he had done what he should have, shared valuable information with the people who needed it. Now he and the gorgeous cop who hated his guts could continue on their separate ways.

Resentment boiled inside her. Robin watched Nate Houston walk away, her grip tightening on the butt of her weapon. She had never wanted to slap handcuffs on someone so badly in her life.

The sight of him dredged up all kinds of bad memories, along with a razor-sharp stab of the heartbreak and confusion she'd lived through.

For a few seconds, she was swallowed up by her past. Five years fell away, reopening a wound of brutal pain, rage, betrayal.

She hadn't thought about her aborted wedding for months, let alone felt its effects, and she resented Nate Houston for making her feel it now. The arrogant infuriating man.

She turned her attention back to Collier. "You were telling me you had finished your walkaround."

He nodded. "The structure is secure if you need to go back inside."

"I don't, but thanks." She had known Houston was back in Oklahoma, just as she had known the fire marshal's office was running the investigation for the small farming community of Warren; she read the paper, after all.

Even so, Robin hadn't imagined she would have to deal with Nate Houston. If for any reason it became necessary to see him again, she would ask Collier to deal with him. McClain was a laid-back, super nice guy. He wouldn't give her any grief for asking such a thing of him.

He shot a look toward Nate's SUV as it drove away. "Have you known Houston long?"

"Long enough," she muttered. "How about you?"

"Since college. We had several fire service training classes together at OSU."

The fact that Collier had asked his friend if he was settling into his house suggested the two of them had spoken with each other at least once since Houston's return.

Robin thought her partner might continue to probe about the other man, but he didn't. She refused to think about Houston for one more second. "What did you find out about our victims, Dennis and Sheila Bane?"

"So far, not much more than they're husband and wife. Both worked outside the home. From my interviews with people at the scene last night, I haven't found anyone who might want to hurt them, but I'll also check at their places of employment."

She knew McClain had spent all night trudging through black, sooty water, and shoveling through ashes and debris. "Once we finish here, I plan to canvass the neighborhood again and re-interview anyone I've already talked to. I'll also do that with the people we interviewed for our first fire-murder. Maybe I'll turn up something."

"I'll take my samples back to the lab and let you know what I find." Collier's green eyes were bloodshot, probably from exhaustion. "The videotape from this fire scene will be ready to view when you want."

"If I learn anything new, I'll call you. Otherwise, I'll plan to see you later today."

After she and Collier split up, Robin spent the day interviewing people who hadn't been available the previous night, as well as the same people she had spoken to before Houston had shown up with his information. Did tonight's victims socialize with her first one? Go to the same church or doctor? High school or college? Did they, or had they ever, worked together?

So far, her answers were no. McClain called mid-afternoon and they agreed she would come by the fire investigator's office to view the videotape after dinner.

She had plans after that to eat with her childhood friends, Terra August Spencer and Meredith Boren

Parrish. Before meeting the fire investigator, she had time to go back to the police department and finish some paperwork on an arrest she had made the day before.

She hadn't eaten since midmorning and her stomach felt hollow. That could be as much as from seeing Nate Houston as from hunger. Deciding it was the latter, she grabbed a protein bar out of the bottom drawer of her desk.

After finishing her forms on the car theft case, she flipped open the file from Presley's first fire murder. She wanted to reread her notes and make sure she didn't miss anything that might connect last April's murders with the one the night before.

"Daly?" Detective Kiley Russell McClain, Collier's wife, called across the squad room. "The captain wants to see you."

"Thanks." Tossing the food wrapper into the trash, Robin made her way across the large room, her low-heeled pumps tapping on city-issue linoleum. She passed rows of putty-colored desks on her way to Hager's office in the far corner.

His blinds were closed, the door open. Just at six feet, the rangy, balding man stood behind his battle-scarred desk. There wasn't a better boss, as far as trusting his detectives to solve their cases without micromanaging them. He had a good sense of humor and a strict sense of justice. John Hager was also one of the best judges of people she'd ever met.

Robin was halfway inside his office when she realized someone else was in the room. She glanced over her left shoulder and froze when her gaze crashed into a deep blue one.

Houston!

She stiffened. What was he doing here?

Standing against the wall, he still wore the pale blue shirt and navy uniform pants that he had that morning. Pants that hinted at the muscular thighs beneath. Fabric stretched across a broad, deep chest and hard shoulders. She didn't remember his shoulders being so wide.

His eyes glittered as he gave her a nod.

She frowned. What was going on? Her gaze shot to Hager.

Her boss slid his hands into the pockets of his gray slacks. "I understand you and Houston met this morning."

They had met a lot longer ago than that, but Robin wasn't saying a word about it. She only nodded.

"I've just gotten off the phone with the chief of police, the fire chief and the state fire marshal."

Something was definitely going on. Robin was uncomfortably aware of Nate standing so close. And the appealing spicy tang of his aftershave.

"Since you two already know each other," Hager continued, "we can dispense with the formalities. Fire Marshal Burke, Fire Chief Wheat and Police Chief Smith agree that these three fire-murders are the work of one guy, a serial arsonist. Houston has experience with other cases like this so he's been put in charge of overseeing a multijurisdictional task force."

Overseeing? Robin froze. "What does that mean exactly?"

"You run everything past him."

"You mean everytime I do anything on my cases?" She couldn't keep the incredulity out of her voice.

Her captain's gaze leveled into hers. "Yes."

Well, yippee.

"McClain is on his way over," Hager said. "The two

of you can catch Houston up on anything you might have learned today."

If she looked at Nate, she wouldn't be able to keep the anger off her face. She took whatever assignment she was given, so she had to work with him.

And for the time being, it looked as though she would be working with the one man with whom she didn't want to share space, let alone information. The man who had convinced her fiancé to leave her standing at the altar. Literally.

Chapter 2

You have got to be kidding!

Robin barely managed to bite back the words. The thought of working with Houston, being under his oversight, had irritation burning through her. It took her a moment to realize Captain Hager was talking.

"Daly, the paperwork authorizing your assignment is finished on my end. The rest will be taken care of by Houston. I need to pick up my daughter at cheerleader camp. If you guys want to use my office to get your ducks in a row, feel free."

He stepped out, leaving Robin alone with Nate. She moved toward one of Hager's visitor's chairs, curling her fingers over the burgundy vinyl back so tight her knuckles ached.

Houston said nothing, but she felt him behind her, his presence making the room seem smaller.

He had stuck his nose in her business five years

earlier, and now he was doing it again. Oh, she knew it wasn't exactly the same—he had no more to say about this than she did—but she was in no frame of mind to be fair. She didn't want to work with him, but that was her tough luck. Until these cases were solved, Nate Houston would be in her business.

This was her job. She could do this. She *would* do this. Still, she practically ground her teeth to dust before she was able to throttle back her blood pressure and face him.

His steady gaze unsettled her. Leaner and harder than she remembered, he braced one shoulder against the opposite wall. The whisker stubble shadowing his jaw looked good on him. Rather than making him appear unkempt, it blunted the stubborn angles of his face. The short sleeves of his uniform shirt skimmed biceps that were solid muscle. Dark hair dusted his forearms, drew her gaze to his strong broad hands. Big hands.

He straightened and took a step toward her. She tensed.

Those blue eyes pierced her. "Look, I know I'm the last person you want to work with."

"We both know 'want to' has nothing to do with it."

"True." Before he could say more, Collier strode into the office.

"Sorry I'm late." Robin's partner carried a manila file folder. "I wanted to wait for some test results."

The band around her chest eased. McClain appeared to have already been told about Houston overseeing their investigations, and he seemed fine with it. Well, why wouldn't he be? Houston hadn't sledge-hammered Collier's life into teeny-tiny pieces.

Catching the knowing glint in Houston's eyes, as if he

expected her to say she couldn't handle it, Robin looked directly at him. "Where do you want to start?"

"How about with McClain's test results?"

She nodded. Listening to her partner's findings would give her a minute to gather her composure.

This was no time to be thinking about Houston and what had happened at her aborted wedding, so she clamped down hard on any thoughts not related to the fire-murders. Too bad she couldn't get rid of Houston himself that easily.

"Tests show the accelerant used last night was the same used in the other fire-murders," McClain said. "It's the Mailman."

"The Mailman?" Nate arched a brow.

Collier chuckled. "Like it? I came up with that moniker while I was running tests on the envelope."

A grin hitched one corner of Nate's mouth and a dimple flashed.

Robin blinked. His face went from intense, almost stern to…charming. Mischievous. Inviting.

Oh, please….

She didn't even like the guy.

She moved to the far corner of Hager's desk, leaving plenty of space between her and Houston. "Any ideas about motive? The victims being burned in their beds is personal, makes it seem like revenge."

"I agree," Nate said. "The sooner we can answer that question, the better. We need to share information, see if we find other things in common besides the arson signature and the cooling-off period."

"Daly and I haven't really had a chance to talk about the time between fires." Collier dragged a hand across his nape. "Why do you think the torch waits twenty-seven days between each one?"

"Maybe he has a job that takes him out of town?" Robin suggested, impatient to leave the small office that put her too close to Nate. "Or one that requires him to work a shift, maybe in another city?"

"Maybe something that puts him in or around Presley every fourth week. Like a job that sends him here instead of taking him out of Presley?"

Collier dragged over one of the visitors' chairs and eased down. "So maybe a job where he works three weeks, is off one week."

"Could it be a salesman?" Robin asked.

Nate shrugged one broad shoulder. "Or someone who travels, giving seminars or teaching classes?"

She folded her arms. "I'll do some research and try to find other jobs that might fit a schedule like that." She looked at Nate. "What about the arsonist you arrested in Chicago? What was his cooling-off period?"

"It was never consistent. At first, the fires were about six weeks apart, then two or three, then less than one."

"What kind of job did your torch have?"

"He worked for the city, the water department."

"Ironic," Robin said at the same time as Nate.

Her gaze shot to his. Despite a slight smile, his blue eyes darkened. The way they had when he had first told her and Collier about the bastard he had put away. Hmm, interesting.

Her partner drummed his fingers on the chair's arm. "The number twenty-seven could be the date of someone's birthday. Or the anniversary of a death, maybe some other traumatic event."

"Shoot," Robin said. "It could be related to phases of the moon for all we know."

"True," Nate muttered, shoving a hand through his thick black hair.

Collier's gaze swung to Robin. "So far, I haven't found anything different about this scene than we did our first one. Daly, did you learn anything new today?"

"I thought I had, but I hit another dead end."

"Do you have a list of who you talked to today?" Nate asked.

"Yes." Did the man think she didn't know how to do her job? Pulling her small notebook from the front pocket of her slacks, she held it out to him.

When Nate reached for it, her grip tightened. He thought he might have to pry it out of her hand. Finally, she released it. He flipped the book open and began skimming pages. Her handwriting was neat and legible. Very detailed, very precise.

After a moment, he pointed to a place on the page. "There's a star next to the name Pattie Roper, then a question mark."

"I was looking for a connection. Our first victim, Les Irwin, dated Pattie about six months ago. The sister of last night's female victim told me the victim suspected her husband of having an affair, but had no idea who the woman might be."

"Hmm," Nate murmured, unable to stop staring at her mouth.

"Anyway," Robin said pointedly, "I figured it couldn't hurt to ask the sister if she'd heard of Pattie Roper, but she hadn't."

"It was a good idea." Forcing his gaze from her, Nate thumbed to the next page in her notebook, glancing at the information. The light scent of soap and woman drifted to him. "Her name never came up in any of the interviews I conducted after my fire-murder. Has anyone's name shown up more than once in either of your investigations?"

"No," Collier said.

Closing Robin's notebook, he returned it, looking at both her and McClain. "I'd like to review your notes on both fires and see if I come across any kind of connection to the arson in Warren."

Collier nodded. "The more information we have, the sooner we can catch this guy."

Noting that Robin's mouth tightened, Nate figured she hated the idea of sharing her files with anyone besides Collier. Still, these investigations needed the expertise of all three of them.

"My files are available to y'all, too," Houston said.

"Even the ones from your big Chicago case?" she challenged.

"Yes, if you think they'll help." He resisted the urge to roll his shoulders and ease the tightness in his muscles.

"My files are back at the fire investigator's office," Collier said.

"Mine are here," Robin offered coolly. "At my desk."

Tension hummed between them and Nate knew she had to feel it, too. He couldn't help but admire her professionalism. She wanted this fire setter as much as he did. Her displeasure at having to work with him was obvious, but she wasn't letting it get in the way.

"What's your next move on the investigation?" he asked her.

"I plan to check swimming pool stores around town and find out in what typical quantities chlorine powder is sold and what month most people start preparing their pools for the summer."

From her rigid stance, Nate figured she thought he meant to tell her to do something else. He had no intention of doing that. "Maybe you'll get lucky and come across someone who purchased the stuff back in April, before our first fire-murder."

He knew he was right when her eyes narrowed slightly, as if she were still waiting for him to tell her how to do her job.

"Of course," she said, "there's the possibility that the suspect could be using chlorine powder left over from last season."

"The stores are a good place to start. I can help you with that. We can split the work."

Surprise flared in her eyes and he read an instant protest in her face, but she only nodded. "Okay."

Collier got to his feet. "Daly and I are planning to look at the videotape of last night's fire scene after dinner. You can join us if you want."

"Thanks, I do."

"All right." The other man stepped toward the door. "Kiley and I are going to grab something to eat. You two want to come?"

"I have some things I need to finish up," Robin said quickly. "Plus I'll start calling places that sell pool chemicals."

"If you're sure your wife won't mind, I'll take you up on dinner," Nate said.

"Great." Collier glanced at Robin. "I'll call when we're finished and the three of us can meet at my office."

"Sounds good."

He started out of the office. When Nate didn't immediately follow, Collier threw a questioning look over his shoulder.

"I'll catch up." Nate flicked a glance at Robin. If there were going to be problems, he wanted to know now.

Collier nodded. "We'll meet you in the parking lot."

As the other man walked off, Nate turned to Robin, not surprised when she edged away. He hadn't been surprised when she declined McClain's offer for supper, either.

Before she could slip out, he pulled his wallet from his back pocket and took out one of his business cards, offering it to her. "McClain already has the numbers where I can be reached, but you'll probably need them, too."

She took the card from him, barely looking at it. He figured he would have to ask for her numbers in return, but before he could, she said, "If you stop at my desk on the way out, I'll give you mine."

"Okay." He caught a whiff of her shampoo as she walked out.

He followed her to the squad room and past several desks before coming to a stop next to hers. Two stacks of files were neatly arranged on one corner with a computer monitor on the other. A framed photograph of Robin standing beside a horse, a black-and-white paint, sat at the desk's center.

Sliding his hands into his pockets, he tilted his head toward the picture. "Your horse?"

"Yes." Reaching into the bottom drawer for her purse, she fished a card from an inside pocket.

He took it, the tips of his fingers grazing hers. A startling jolt of heat moved up his arm. When he saw the pulse in her neck jerk, he knew she'd felt it, too. Whatever the hell *it* was.

After returning her handbag to its place, she slid two

files from the top of a stack. "These are my files on the Mailman fires. Do you want them now?"

"Unless you'd rather bring them to Collier's office."

"I'll do that. It will give me time to make copies."

"Okay. See ya in an hour or so."

She sure didn't give an inch. She turned away, starting toward the other side of the room. As far as he was concerned, they still had business. He lightly touched her elbow and she spun.

The fierce look on those delicate features said he was lucky to still have his hand.

Whoa. "Are you going to have a problem working with me?"

"Not unless you make it one." Her blue eyes glittered like ice. "And we both know it doesn't matter if either of us have a problem with it. We still have to do our jobs."

"I don't know about you, but I'd like to feel as though I'm not a target every day when I come to work."

A slight flush spread across her cheeks. "Fair enough."

He nodded, slipping her card into the pocket of his uniform shirt. "I'll see you later this evening then."

"All righty."

All righty. As he walked out, he felt her stare boring into his back as though to make sure he really did leave.

Working with her was not at the top of his wish list, either, but she was right. They were both professionals; they needed to do the job without their personal feelings interfering.

He hoped she was finished making it personal. Her suggestion that he might have put away the wrong guy in the Chicago case had resentment churning in his gut, but he wasn't going to let Detective Gorgeous make him doubt himself or a solid case, a *closed* case.

She had taken the news of their working together better than he had expected. He was still in one piece. Even so, Nate had no illusions that things would get any easier between him and the petite brunette.

An hour after viewing the fire scene videotape with Collier and Nate, Robin joined Terra Spencer and Meredith Parrish for dinner at her house. Upon arriving, she briefly wished that she could be alone, maybe take her horse out for a long ride. But the second she saw her friends, she was glad they were there.

She had finally wrapped her head around working with Houston. It had helped that he had treated her and Collier as partners and not as people who had to report to him. Still, that didn't mean she liked the idea of working with him any better than she had before. He seriously unsettled her. Why had he moved back to Oklahoma anyway?

After dinner, the three women stayed seated around the light oak dining table. Robin poured herself another glass of merlot, noticing when her friends exchanged a puzzled look.

"What's going on?" Terra frowned, sweeping her golden-red hair over one shoulder. "You're on your second glass of wine."

"You'll never guess who asked for my phone number today."

"It can't be anyone good." Meredith wore her blonde curls in a chic twist, as she usually did, while seeing patients at Presley Medical Center, where she was a doctor on staff. "You usually don't drink two glasses of wine in one night."

"So, spill." Terra sipped at her tea.

Robin knew the other women weren't having alcohol because they both had to drive home. After another sip of wine, she said, "Nate Houston."

Both of her friends started visibly. Some of Terra's drink sloshed out onto the table and she grabbed a napkin to clean it up. "What!"

"He's got some nerve." Concern shadowed Meredith's blue eyes. "Why would he ask for your number?"

Robin laughed. "He didn't ask because he wanted to. He caught a fire-murder similar to the ones Collier and I are working and today he was assigned to oversee our cases."

"That answers my question about whether the bigwigs are aware that they could be dealing with a serial arsonist." Terra was Presley's first female fire investigator, and had trained Collier.

"So, how was it seeing him?" Meredith asked quietly.

Terra's green eyes darkened. "Did he act like a jerk?"

"No." Robin would've liked to say yes, but he had remained completely professional. So far, he hadn't been the hard-ass she had expected.

She might be resigned to working with the man; that didn't mean she was suddenly all soft and gooey about him. "Tomorrow will be the real kickoff for the task force. I'll start to get a better feel for him then. He wants Collier and me to go to his crime scene, see if we can find something he didn't."

Meredith gave her a thoughtful look. "You could ask to be reassigned."

"Wouldn't he love that?" Robin drawled. "No way. I'm not about to let him think I can't handle it."

"Do you think he feels the same about working with you?"

Surprised, Robin paused. "I don't know. I never thought about it. You'd think he might at least feel a little awkward after what he did, but if he does, I can't tell."

Meredith shook her head. "I'll never understand why he talked Kyle out of the wedding, or even how he did it."

Neither would Robin. That September day seemed so long ago, yet every second was excruciatingly clear in her mind.

She had really believed Kyle Emrick was Mr. Right. They had hit it off from the beginning, when he had transferred from the El Reno Police Department to Presley P.D. After dating a year, they became engaged.

On a fall day six months later, she had been in the anteroom at the church with her mom, waiting to walk down the aisle with her dad. Memories rushed back—her excitement, the little flutter of nerves.

Just as she had picked up her bouquet, Kyle walked in saying he needed to talk to her. He couldn't marry her, he said. Nate Houston had convinced him it was wrong. Disbelieving at first, she had actually laughed and told him to stop joking around. Nate Houston had nothing to say about Kyle marrying her.

But her fiancé kept insisting that Houston was right; it would be a bad idea for Kyle to marry her. As if Houston were the pope and he had issued some ridiculous decree.

It wasn't until Kyle told her to return his wedding

band that Robin believed him. She'd been numb and dazed. Lost. By the time her father had explained to the guests that the wedding was off, she was furious. At Kyle. At Nate.

She had gone in search of Houston, but he had disappeared. No big surprise. He'd done his damage. Why hang around?

Who the hell did he think he was? Why had her fiancé let himself be swayed by the guy? They were friends, but not brothers. Not even fraternity brothers. Over the next twelve months, Robin had asked Kyle repeatedly to give her his reasons for calling off the wedding, but he wouldn't. She wanted answers and she had considered asking Nate, but she didn't trust him to tell her.

On what would've been her and Kyle's one-year anniversary, she asked for the last time. All he would say was that he still believed it would've been wrong for them to marry. A month later, he had transferred to the traffic division and a year after that, Robin had been assigned to homicide.

In the three years since, she had moved past her hurt, moved past the anger. Evidently, her resentment against Houston was another matter.

Even if she had dodged a bullet, she wasn't thanking Nate Houston for it. He'd been witness to—*party to*—the most humiliating day of her life.

Meredith frowned. "Nate was the groomsman who was supposed to walk with me. I remember hearing him say his marriage had hit a rocky patch and he was trying to work things out with his wife. Do you know if he did?"

"Nope." What kind of woman would marry a man like Nate Houston? A man who went around interfering with things that were none of his business. Life-altering things.

Robin realized Collier hadn't asked Nate about a wife any of the times they had all been together today. For some reason, she didn't think he had a spouse any longer. He just seemed…alone.

Terra pushed her plate to the side. "Since you never found out from Kyle exactly why he called off the wedding, do you plan to ask Nate what he said to the jerk?"

Robin snorted. "I've lived through that humiliation once, thank you very much. I'm not doing it again. The only things I'm talking to Houston about are murders and fires."

Tomorrow she would find out how this alliance would work, what kind of manager and investigator Houston was.

"I wouldn't dredge it all back up, either," Meredith said.

The doctor had relived her own devastation when she had to accept the news that the ex-fiancé she believed to be dead was very much alive.

Terra and Robin had both expressed misgivings about Meredith reuniting with her ex, Gage Parrish, but he now seemed like a different person, at least as far as the way he treated Meredith. They had been married fourteen months, and so far, she was number one with him, period.

It was that way for Terra, too. Her cop husband, Jack Spencer, worshiped the woman.

Robin was happy for her friends, but she didn't expect or need to ever find such commitment for herself. It wasn't only because her friends had found two of the last good men on earth. She wasn't willing to endure the hell Meredith in particular had gone through to get there.

"Let's change the subject." Robin smiled at the other two women. "Tell me how things are going with y'all."

"Oh, I have a new family picture." Terra went into the living room and snagged her purse from the taupe suede sofa, returning to the kitchen as Meredith gathered up the plates.

The blonde stacked the dishes on the counter next to the sink. "Gage's business is really taking off. He hired another investigator last week."

Parrish had been a fire investigator with the Oklahoma City Fire Department before the U.S. Marshals faked his death. The brutally long hours and his own single-minded focus had been what came between him and Meredith before he was put into Witness Security.

When things had worked out so that he was free to return to his old life, he had opened his own private fire investigation company so he could choose his workload and adjust his hours around Meredith's hospital schedule. He had kept his promise.

Terra handed a photograph to Robin. Meredith returned to the table, bending to look at the picture. Terra, Jack and Elise looked insanely happy. Terra's tall, dark-haired husband held her close with one arm and held their daughter in the other. The toddler was planting a kiss on his cheek.

Robin smiled. "This goes on the fridge with the others."

"Same here." Meredith put one of the photos on the counter, near her purse, to take home.

The three of them had been friends since junior high, when Meredith and Robin had moved to Presley. Robin was much closer to them than to her own sister, Wendy. Most of the time she didn't even know what her hard-partying sister was up to.

She glanced at Meredith. "Have you and Gage talked about starting a family?"

"We want to have a year to ourselves first."

"That's a good idea." Terra slid back into her chair and folded one long leg under her. "It worked out great for Jack and me to have some 'couple' time."

As Robin caught up with her friends, she found her thoughts wandering to the investigation. To Houston. Something he had said both that morning and that evening niggled at her. Something about the last big case he had closed in Chicago, the one where he might have put away the wrong man. Both times the subject had come up, there had been a flash of raw emotion in his eyes.

Robin could have sworn it was pain. But why?

Realizing where her thoughts had gone, she pushed away her questions. Why should she care about anything in Nate Houston's eyes? All she wanted was to solve these cases. The sooner that happened, the sooner she could get away from him.

Chapter 3

Just after eight o'clock the next morning, Nate waited for Robin and Collier at the training center complex located less than a mile from I-35. The three of them had agreed to meet there and ride in one car to Warren. The complex was fairly new and included buildings for administration, classroom space and the drill tower, used for practicing various fire procedures.

June heat shimmered around him. He leaned against the side of his SUV, one ankle crossed over the other, as he spoke to the secretary at the fire marshal's office, telling her where he would be today.

He hadn't known what to expect out of Daly last night, when they had met at Collier's office to view the tape from their latest fire scene, but things had gone well. She had kept her distance, and afterwards she probably hadn't given him a single thought. Too bad he couldn't say the same. He had thought about her a lot, and not once in the context of the investigation. He didn't understand it.

Hell, Nate never even thought about the women he was seeing unless he was with them.

Since his divorce three years earlier from Stephanie, he was interested in only short-term flings, one or two nights then he moved on. Nate didn't want a committed relationship. He had failed at that.

Now for some reason, he couldn't *stop* thinking about Robin. Wondering if the petite detective was involved with anyone, if she had been involved at all since breaking up with Kyle. Nate knew three things about her. She liked horses, liked her job and had been engaged before. That was it. And he wanted to know more.

As if she would ever tell him. Hell, she would probably be offended if he tried to get on friendly terms with her. He bet Robin Daly could squash his curiosity inside of two seconds when she arrived. One look from those cool, disdainful eyes would shift his mind back where it should be.

A dark blue sedan drove up and Nate concluded his phone call, straightening as Robin parked in the space next to his. If she knew he had been thinking about her, she would probably blow a gasket. The idea made him grin.

She climbed out of her car, cell phone to her ear. She settled her sunglasses on her head.

Holding up a finger to show him she would be just a minute, she turned away slightly. She looked cool and professional in a pink sleeveless top and navy slacks, but it was her hair that had him going still inside.

She wore it down, sliding around her shoulders like a thick curtain of satin. Stunning. It was a deep, rich brown, sable. As glossy as hot silk. He wanted to touch it.

The way it was pulled up at the sides drew attention to the classic lines of her profile. He didn't know why the relaxed hairstyle made such a difference. Maybe because it made her appear softer, more *touchable*. He didn't need to be thinking about touching her, or anything on her.

She flipped her cell phone shut and turned, shoulders rigid. "Looks like we'll have to reschedule."

"Did you catch another case?"

"No, that was McClain. He was just called in to court."

Ah, she didn't want to go alone with Nate. Not his favorite scenario, either. "Will he be on call all day?"

He already knew the answer. He'd done his share of waiting to be called to the witness stand.

"Yes. We'll have to go another day."

"He could be there for a week."

"I guess so."

"We don't have a week," Nate said evenly. "Not if we want to catch this torch before he kills someone else."

"You said you wanted both me and McClain to look at your crime scene."

"That would be my preference." *Believe me,* he thought. "But I don't think we should wait. I want you for more than a fresh pair of eyes. As a cop, you might pick up on something I didn't."

She hesitated, which got to him. "You said you weren't going to have a problem working with me."

Her eyes narrowed. "I don't."

"If your not wanting to go to Warren isn't work-related, it must be personal." He knew being with him bugged her and that bugged *him*. He folded his arms. "You afraid to be alone with me, Daly?"

"Give me a break." Blue fire sparked in her eyes.

Was she going to hold that incident against him forever? He'd done her a favor. Kyle was still a cop in the Presley P.D., so Robin had to know about him, had to know just how great a favor Nate had done her.

"What else am I supposed to think?" he asked. "You're the cop on this investigation. Want me to request someone else?"

"Don't you dare." Her voice was low, fierce. "This is my case, Houston. I'm working it."

"If McClain were here, you wouldn't have a problem going."

"Maybe I just like him better than you."

"That's because you haven't spent any time with me," he said with a grin.

She didn't smile, just stared, her eyes growing more remote. He was going to have to start over with her, declare another truce. Great. Would it be like this every time he saw her? "It's an hour drive. Surely you can stand my company that long."

"You're right. Sorry." She looked at him across the top of her vehicle. "Whose car do you want to take?"

Nate blinked. *What the hell?* "Uh, mine. More leg-room."

"Okay." She opened the back door of her car and pulled out a lightweight jacket in the same navy as her slacks.

Draping it over one arm, she dropped her keys into her black shoulder bag as she walked to the passenger side of Nate's SUV. He noticed her badge and holster clipped on to the waistband of her pants. Today, he carried his gun in a clip-on holster, too.

Nate slid behind the wheel, his nerves twitching as though he'd had too much caffeine. He had been fine until learning he would be making this trip alone with Robin.

As he got behind the wheel, her light wildflower scent drifted to him. He noticed her slowly looking him over and adrenaline shot through him like a drug. When she realized he had noticed, her gaze changed to wintry and laser-sharp.

Ah, there it was. The look of contempt guaranteed to put him in his place. She acted as though he had a contagious disease, It bugged the hell out of him.

He figured she wouldn't talk to him unless she absolutely had to. He could live with that.

As he drove out of the complex, he again felt her watching him.

"You have a gun."

"So do you."

"I'm a cop," she said flatly. "I assume you have a permit to carry."

"Yes. All agents at the fire marshal's office are sworn peace officers."

"You can arrest people too?"

He nodded.

"Hmm, I didn't know that."

He merged onto I-35, going north. They rode in silence for a few minutes. Stealing a look at her, Nate traced the lush curve of her breasts, slid down the lean thighs beneath the slim navy slacks. He bet she had great legs. He had never seen her in anything besides pants and a wedding dress.

Small hoops in her ears emphasized dainty lobes and the satiny curve of her neck. Her lightly tanned skin was flawless, fine-grained and petal-smooth. From touching her arm last night, he knew how soft her skin was, knew her lips would be just as soft.

And then there was her hair. He still wanted to get his hands in it, mess it up.

She caught him looking at her and arched a brow, frost gathering in her yes.

He got the message, but he didn't look away. She had drawn the line and he had no intention of stepping over it. That didn't mean he couldn't look if he wanted. And he wanted.

He accelerated past a van. "The victim, Brad Myers, owned a restaurant. He's survived by an ex-wife and two kids. And a brother. They didn't get along very well."

"I certainly understand that." She slipped her sunglasses back on.

Knowing her sister, Nate got it, too. From the little bit he knew of both of them, two women couldn't be more different. Robin, smart and steady. Wendy, wild and selfish.

"Was the brother ever a suspect?"

Nate shook his head. "His alibi checked out, and I couldn't find a motive."

"He wasn't a beneficiary in Brad's will or insurance policy?"

"No."

"Who are the beneficiaries?"

"The victim's ex-wife and his kids. The guy lived over the restaurant, so the fire destroyed his residence as well as his business."

"Did you find any prints at the scene?"

"No." He changed lanes to pass a semitrailer. "I called a few swimming pool stores last night."

"Busy man. Any luck?"

"None of the people I spoke to could tell a difference

in sales of pool chemicals until May, when they took a big jump."

"That's well after the date of our first fire-murder."

"Yeah."

Nate found himself wondering if she had ever come close again to getting married, but he wasn't asking. The less personal they kept their time together, the better.

"So, Houston, why did you come back to Oklahoma?"

His gaze shot to her. So much for not getting personal.

"The job offer was too good to pass up?"

Nate wasn't sure what surprised him more: that she had asked about something besides the investigation, or that she had initiated the conversation.

"My stepdad passed away suddenly about nine months ago. I wanted to be near my mom."

"Is she getting to the age where she needs help?"

"She's fine, but my sister has three kids. If something happens and my mom does need help, it isn't fair to expect Becca to be available all the time."

Robin eyed him speculatively.

"What? You can't believe I have a mother? Did you think I was hatched?"

"No." She continued to study him. "You have a sister."

He nodded. "She's two years older than I am."

He took the highway exit that led to the rural community of Warren. The service road curved through hills and woods for a couple of miles before reaching town.

"What about your dad?" Robin asked.

"What about him?"

"I looked up some articles about that big arson case

you worked in Chicago. You said eighteen people died in the nursing home blaze, three of them firefighters."

Where was she going with this? The muscles in his shoulders knotted tighter. He could just imagine how she would react if he started with the questions.

"The articles I read listed one of the victims as a Charles Houston. Was he a relative?"

"My dad." Nate's voice sounded rough, gravelly. He hadn't talked about this in a long time, and he didn't want to talk about it now. A dull ache lodged under his ribs.

He waited for her to rip into him with something like, "Maybe that's why you can't objectively determine if you put away the wrong guy."

"I'm sorry. That had to be rough."

Nate was so startled his hand jerked on the wheel. She sounded sincere. He wasn't sure exactly what to make of her bringing up the subject, but he had to give her credit for not taking a shot at him. "Thanks," he murmured.

Since she had crossed into personal territory, Nate thought about asking her if she had come to terms with Kyle and what had happened. Kyle had sworn he had told Robin the reason he called off the wedding. She had to be glad she hadn't married the guy, so why did she act as though she were still angry at Nate?

He wasn't going to ask. Besides, their personal lives were the last thing they should be talking about.

The two-lane road led them into Warren, and Nate took the first right turn. The streets were old and cracked, wide enough for at least four cars side-by-side. Faded red-brick buildings with flat facades and weathered store fronts lined the street on both sides. The town had a quaint and quiet charm.

Nate parked in front of the police department, which looked newer than the other buildings. He climbed out of the SUV and adjusted his holster. As Robin pulled on her jacket, she stepped with Nate into the air-conditioned glass-front office. Chief Bolen left one of the office's two computers to shake Nate's hand and meet Robin.

The gray-haired man towered above both of them. He had sharp features, with deep laugh lines around his mouth. After telling the chief their reason for coming, the older lawman accompanied them to the restaurant, a block down and one over, still surrounded by crime scene tape.

The two-story structure had burned to the ground and the acrid odors of charred wood and melted plastic still lingered. Robin walked around the building.

Nate showed her the point of origin. Pulling a small notebook from her jacket pocket, she jotted a few notes before they moved on toward the home of the victim's brother, Billy Myers.

As they walked from the center of town, they passed a gas station and convenience store. Nate and Robin filled Bolen in about the third fire-murder and their suspicions that they were dealing with a serial arsonist.

The convenience store fronted a residential area of small, older homes. They knocked on the door of a small, white frame house. It was answered by a glowering concrete block of a man.

Nate showed his badge. "Mr. Myers, Agent Houston. Do you remember me?"

"Yeah. You're from the fire marshal's office." He wasn't drunk, but did reek of alcohol. Looking sullen, he ran a hand through his long, combed-back hair. "Did you find out who set the fire that burned down my brother's restaurant?"

"Not yet." Nate gestured to Robin. "This is Detective Daly. She's working the case with me."

Billy's gaze slid over her. "She's a lot prettier than you are."

Nate waited for Robin to turn her glacial stare on the other man.

Instead, she took off her sunglasses and smiled. "I know you've already spoken to Agent Houston and Chief Bolen, but could you spare me a few moments?"

"Sure."

"Is there anything else you remember?"

He shook his head, his gaze tracking over her body, one inch at a time.

Nate shifted slightly, his eyes narrowing at the man in warning.

She didn't react to the man's leering. "Maybe something you saw or heard? Anything?"

Myers started to shake his head again, then paused. "Well, there was a woman."

Nate frowned. "What woman?"

"The night before the fire, I saw a woman sneaking out of Brad's apartment and I asked him about her. Since his divorce, he's been entertaining a lot of women. He said he didn't know her name."

"They just hooked up for one night?" Nate asked.

Billy shrugged. "That's what it sounded like."

This was the first Nate had heard about any woman with Brad Myers the night before the fire. "Why didn't you mention this either of the times I talked to you?"

He smiled at Robin. "I clean forgot about it until your pretty partner asked me."

"Do you have a description?" she asked.

The man thought for a minute. "She was real skinny. Her hair wasn't as long as yours, maybe to her jaw. I couldn't tell the color. You could ask around town, see if anyone else knew about her and Brad. In a town this size, somebody might have."

"Do you think you might recognize her if you saw her again?" Nate asked as Robin jotted more notes.

"I don't know. It was dark. Brad's outside light was busted."

Robin glanced up. "Where would they have met?"

"Brad's restaurant, The Gemini. Or maybe the bar on the other side of town."

"Thanks." She took a card from her purse and gave it to Billy. "If you think of anything else, could you call me?"

"Yes, ma'am. Be real happy to do that."

She smiled as she started back up the street with Nate and the chief.

Billy called out, "Maybe that woman's the one who set the fire."

Maybe, but Nate didn't think so. Judging from the skepticism on Daly's face, she didn't either.

"Or maybe it was Janine, Brad's ex," the victim's brother suggested. "If she thought he was having an affair, maybe she decided to get back at him."

"Thanks!" Robin slipped on her shades, glancing at Nate.

He shook his head. "I looked at the ex-wife, but she had an alibi. Even if she hadn't, nothing else lined up. This case is too similar to the others. It has to be the same arsonist."

"I agree."

"So, no connection to Les Irwin's ex-girlfriend, Pattie Roper, or the woman who may have been having an affair with Dennis Bane."

"No connection that we've found *yet*," Robin reminded.

"Right."

They spent the next couple of hours talking to people, asking if anyone knew about the mystery woman who had been with Brad Myers the night before the fire. Myers' ex-wife, the mayor, merchants, the two postal employees. No one knew about her.

Nate couldn't help being impressed by Robin. She read people well, remained calm. The tension between the two of them could easily have affected these interviews, but she didn't let it. The case came first with her. Nate admired that.

That wasn't all he admired, he admitted to himself, as his gaze traced the slender lines of her back, the gentle flare of her hips. His attention again went to her hair.

Her back-off attitude hadn't lessened his desire to get his hands in the silky mass. It hadn't gotten rid of his curiosity about her, either. With a jolt, he realized Detective Gorgeous had held his attention longer than any woman since his ex-wife.

Saturday morning found Robin at the softball field on the north side of Presley. Today was the annual softball matchup between Presley's fire and police departments, a charity event that raised money for the families of firefighters and police officers killed in the line of duty.

In a navy P.P.D. T-shirt, shorts and ball cap, she warmed up with Kiley McClain along a stretch of chain-link fence that paralleled the first base line. Robin always enjoyed this game and she would enjoy this one more than most because she didn't have to see Nate Houston.

After spending a good part of the previous day with him, she was glad for the space. Their trip had gone surprisingly well. Half-expecting him to take over at any minute, to insert himself into interviews where she neither needed nor wanted his help, she had been surprised when he hadn't. Except for asking Billy Myers why he hadn't told Nate about the woman seen coming out of the victim's apartment, Nate had let Robin run the show.

Though she would never admit it, he had been right when he accused her of not wanting to be alone with him. Collier's canceling at the last minute had thrown her.

Both she and Houston had been professional. She hadn't anticipated anything else, but she also hadn't imagined they would work together as smoothly as they had. While she didn't want to give that too much weight, it was good for the investigation.

Another thing that surprised her was that she couldn't stop thinking about the emotion on his face when she had asked about his father dying in the nursing home fire. The bleakness in his eyes had compassion welling inside her. She didn't want to feel anything for Houston, but she knew the heavy hollowness of loss and how it shrouded your life. Robin would never have guessed they had anything in common.

"Looks like we're going to have a good crowd today." Kiley pointed over Robin's shoulder.

She looked, noting the bleachers were quickly filling. When she turned back, Collier was standing behind Kiley, his head bent to hers. He wore a red Presley fire department T-shirt and shorts, like the rest of his teammates. He said something only she could hear.

His red-haired wife blushed and jabbed him in the stomach with her elbow. "Get out of here."

He grinned, kissing her neck before he walked over to the fence. "We're going to kick your butts, ladies."

"Dream on, McClain." His wife's eyes sparkled.

As Kiley and Robin continued to throw the ball, Collier turned his attention to her. "Anything new on the case?"

"No. Just what I told you about the mystery woman when I called last night."

"That was good work."

"We got lucky, but we're not having that same luck with the swimming pool stores."

"How was the trip with Houston?"

Robin fumbled the ball, managing to keep it in her glove. Why was he bringing up Nate? "It was fine."

"He was pretty impressed that you got some new information."

"Then my work on earth is done," she drawled. Houston had complimented her? Robin had to admit she wasn't being nearly as nice as he was.

Collier grinned.

"To your dugouts!" Jack Spencer called out.

Robin and Kiley jogged over to join the other cops. Robin waved at Terra, who sat in the bleachers with hers and Jack's daughter, Elise.

The dark-haired little girl bounced in Terra's lap, calling in her baby voice, "Daddy, Daddy!"

Jack smiled at her, then turned back to the team. "We're in the field first."

They all took their places amid cheers and calls from the audience. Robin and Kiley played second base and shortstop, respectively. Spencer pitched and Clay Jessup was at first base, with Captain Hager at third.

"Batter up!" the umpire called.

Robin took her position, calling encouragement over her shoulder to the people playing the field behind her.

From the corner of her eye, she noticed someone moving to home plate and she shifted her gaze to the batter. Her mouth went dry.

Nate Houston. What was he doing here? Who had invited him? And wow, he looked good. At the sight of his long-lined athletic frame, something clutched hard and deep in her belly.

He wore a gray sweatshirt with the sleeves cut out. Her gaze moved over bronze, steel-hard biceps, to large hands and down to powerful, hair-dusted legs. The loose fabric of the shirt did nothing to disguise how defined and muscular his chest was beneath. He was all hard angles, planes and sleek sinew.

Hers was a purely physical reaction. She'd known the guy was in shape, but *yowsa*.

"Hubba hubba," Kiley said under her breath.

Robin grinned. "You're married, McClain. You better simmer down."

The other woman laughed. "I was talking about my husband. Who did you think I was talking about?"

It took considerable effort to force her gaze away from Houston, but when she did, she saw Collier standing only a couple of feet from the other man. She hadn't noticed McClain at all. Nate Houston had short-circuited her system. The only signal getting to her brain was *yes, yes, yes*.

Kiley gave her a sly look. "Not hard to guess who you're looking at."

Robin felt her face flame; she hoped her friend would believe it was from the heat. She tugged her cap down, ignoring the knowing glint in her friend's eyes. "Let's get this show on the road!"

Houston didn't swing the bat until the third pitch. He slammed the ball into left field, making it to second base before the ball was thrown to Robin. He was safe, so she returned the ball to Spencer.

Nate stood on her right, poised to run, with one foot on the bag. "Hey, Daly."

"Hey." Unable to squash her curiosity, she asked, "How did you know about the game?"

"McClain invited me. He said it wouldn't matter that I don't work for PFD, since this event is for charity."

"Right." This close she caught the scents of soap and man. And she could see those biceps were every bit as granite-hard as they had looked from home plate.

Pulling her gaze away, she focused on Collier, the next batter. Spencer's pitch shot straight into the strike zone.

"Very nice," she murmured. "Perfect."

"It was inside, low," Nate declared.

She made a sound. "Get some glasses, Houston."

Jack sailed his next pitch over the plate.

"Another one inside and low," Nate said.

Robin sent him a disbelieving look. "Dude, it was dead center."

A grin tugged at his lips. "I'm not the one who needs glasses."

"I can't even imagine how you saw your own ball well enough to hit it, Grandpa."

He laughed outright then, a rich baritone that shook something loose inside Robin. "We'll see how you do when you get up to bat, Daly. Maybe we can find you a Seeing Eye dog."

"Aren't you adorable?" she drawled, biting back a smile.

Jack gave Nate a hard-eyed stare then faced forward and fired in another pitch. *Smack!* Collier hit the ball high over Robin's head. The spectators jumped to their feet, whistling and cheering. Houston took off for third base, reaching it seconds before the center fielder managed to throw the ball to Kiley, who fired it to Captain Hager.

As Spencer geared up for the next batter, Robin found herself watching Nate, who stood on the edge of third base. When she realized she was staring, she refocused her attention on the game. The firefighters scored three runs before the cops earned their next time at bat.

Jerry French, a veteran firefighter, pitched for their team while Nate caught. Robin was third at bat and walked to the plate in the midst of deafening cheers for French's three perfect pitches to the previous player.

As she lined up over the plate, Houston stood just in front of her and lobbed the ball to the pitcher. She tried not to notice the flex of muscle and sinew in his arms and shoulders.

He lifted his mask, blue eyes twinkling. "Good luck, Daly."

She narrowed her eyes. "Don't even think about messing with me."

He chuckled. Waiting for the first pitch, she was nervous. She wouldn't put it past him to do something at the last second, like yell and startle her.

Nate caught the first pitch, high and outside, without saying a word.

The next pitch was called as a low ball. She began to relax. Hearing Terra and Elise cheering in the background, Robin assumed her stance.

She kept her eye on the ball. Perfect. Just as she started to swing, she heard a low, smoky voice, "Nice legs, Daly."

Startled, her jaw dropped. The ball zoomed past, right into Houston's mitt. Her gaze jerking to him, she glared.

"Strike one!" the umpire called.

"Dirty pool, Houston," she said in a low voice. "Don't make me use this bat on you."

"Okay, okay." Lips curving, he raised one hand in surrender.

"No more heckling."

"That was a compliment." Amusement traced his words. "Want me to take it back?"

"I want you to play the game," she muttered.

He laughed, signaling Jerry that he was ready for the next pitch.

Robin got a solid hit, bringing in a runner and making it to third base herself. Her team was behind by one run when they took the field again.

Back at second base, Robin tried to concentrate on the game. When it was again Houston's turn to bat, the bases were loaded. She wished she could throw him off balance the way he had done her, but she couldn't do anything from her position. She would have to settle for tagging him out. She really wanted that.

He took his sweet time choosing a pitch. When he hit it, the ball sailed to right field. He had passed first and was on his way to second when the ball reached Clay, who fired it to Robin.

She caught it just as Houston slid into second base. Right between her legs. She barely managed to keep herself from stumbling.

"Safe!" the umpire called.

Frozen, her glove hanging uselessly at her side, Robin stared down at the man lying at her feet.

He propped himself on one elbow, staring at her legs with an arrested look on his face. Was he looking at her scar? Her skin tingled. Her senses sharpened. She noticed how his hair curled slightly on the ends. The streak of blood down the side of his arm. His sweat-dampened shirt clinging to his broad chest.

His gaze lifted to hers and tension arced between them. The crowd's cheers faded into the background. Why wasn't he moving?

Why wasn't *she?*

Her brain kicked in and she frowned at him. "Are you all right?"

"I'm fine." His attention dropped to the length of her leg bared by her shorts. "Just enjoying the view."

Oh, my gosh. Heat shimmered beneath her skin and that got her moving. She nudged him with one foot. "Get up!"

Grinning, he rolled to his feet as she took a step back. The crowd continued clapping and cheering.

"Good catch," he said. "You almost got me."

"Next time I will." What was she saying? She didn't want a next time.

One corner of his mouth hitched up as if he knew what she was thinking. "I take back what I said earlier," he murmured.

"About what?"

"Your legs aren't nice, they're great."

Her eyes narrowed. He was just trying to get to her. There was no time to reply. The ball was hit and he sprinted for third base. Clay tagged the batter out at first then fired the ball to third just as Houston started for home. He slid into the bag, but the catcher snagged the ball and touched Nate a millisecond before he reached home plate.

"Out!" the ump called.

Getting to his feet, Nate good-naturedly accepted the umpire's call. He walked to his team's dugout, brushing red dirt off his arms before catching a bottle of water someone tossed to him and taking a long drink.

Robin couldn't pull her gaze from the play of muscles in his arms. Why couldn't she stop looking at him? Hadn't she seen enough of him already? Yesterday. Today. Something weird was going on with her and she didn't like it.

It was then she realized that, for the first time while being around him, she hadn't thought about her aborted wedding at all.

Because she'd been thinking about Houston!

No man had ever affected her in such a strongly physical way. If it had been only lust, Robin could've handled it, but this warmth, this buoyancy in her chest was worse than lust.

Nate Houston had talked her fiancé into not marrying her, and she still didn't know why. And here she was, afraid she could actually like this guy.

Chapter 4

Robin didn't want to like Nate Houston. He had ruined her wedding. That reminder should've been enough to put him out of her mind, but Monday morning, she was still thinking about him.

It was because he was different than what she had expected. And because of the startling unwanted desire that had slammed into her like a bullet when he had shown up on Saturday at the ball field. She hadn't been prepared to see him let alone drool over his jock-of-the-month look.

Today she was ready. She could appreciate his dark appeal without wanting to go deeper inside the man. When they were together, it was all about business. Like now, as they arrived at Dennis Bane's place of employment in downtown Oklahoma City.

Collier was still on call for court, which meant it would be only Robin and Nate trying to find out if anyone might have a reason to kill their third fire-murder victim and his wife.

Nate had met Robin at the police department before nine that morning, and they had ridden together in his SUV. They both wore some semblance of a uniform. Nate's navy polo shirt sported the emblem of the fire marshal's office, and he wore his badge clipped to the trim waist of his dark blue slacks. His gun was tucked into his pants at the small of his back.

Her badge and holster were clipped to the waistband of her dusky blue slacks, just below the hem of a matching sleeveless top.

When they stepped out of the vehicle, heat rolled over them like a tide. Adjusting her sunglasses, Robin walked with Houston into the foyer of the high-rise.

Cool air swirled around them as they walked across the dark, gold-veined marble floor toward a bank of elevators. A waist-high podium against one wall of elevators held an electronic listing of the building's tenants.

Robin and Nate stopped there, her gaze skimming the directory.

"There it is, Eastman and Associates," Nate said.

She followed the direction of his finger. The commercial leasing and management company was on floor fifteen. Reached by a glass elevator. Vertigo and glass elevators did not mix.

"Yippee," she muttered.

"What's that?" Nate glanced over as he punched the up button.

"Nothing." She thought longingly of taking the stairs, but she wouldn't. Not only because it was impractical, but also because she didn't want to show any weakness, not in front of Houston. As long as she kept her eyes trained on the steel doors or the floor she would be fine.

The elevator stopped several times on the way up and Robin had no problems. They reached their floor and stepped out. Just a few feet away was a large glass door identified by black lettering as the office of Eastman and Associates.

As Nate reached to open the door, Robin stopped. For a moment, she had almost forgotten he was "in charge." "How do you want to handle the interviews?"

He frowned. "What would you do if Collier were here?"

"I'd probably lead."

"Let's do it that way then."

"Okay." Excellent. This might go better than she had anticipated. He wasn't trying to muscle in on anything. Though glad, she wondered why. Meddling seemed to be his MO.

Nate opened the heavy door and followed Robin inside. Dark hardwood floors gleamed. Lush area rugs in a muted green and cream complemented the dark green leather sofa and the pairs of chairs that flanked each end, making the area inviting and open. The receptionist's desk was also done in dark wood and the privacy counter along the top was crowded with plants and bouquets of flowers. From the sympathy card on a basket of ivy, Robin assumed the arrangements had been sent with condolences on the death of Dennis Bane.

"May I help you?" The blonde behind the desk was young, maybe twenty. Her brown eyes were red-rimmed, as if she had been crying.

Robin showed her badge. "Detective Daly, Presley P.D. This is Agent Houston with the fire marshal's office. We'd like to talk to the person in charge."

"That's Mr. Eastman." The woman picked up the phone and hit a button on a multiline receiver, speaking quietly to the person on the other end. After a couple of minutes, a tall silver-haired man appeared in the entrance that led to the offices. His black suit was perfectly tailored to his lean frame. The fabric looked expensive, as did the shoes that were polished to a military sheen.

Distinguished and sharp-eyed, he extended his hand to Robin. "David Eastman."

After introductions, Robin explained the reason for their visit. "We're investigating the fire that killed Mr. and Mrs. Bane. We'd like to talk to you and your employees. It's standard procedure."

"Whatever you need. I have a large conference room not being used at the moment, if you would prefer people to come to you."

"No need for that. Their offices will be fine." Robin wanted to see if anything in individual work spaces showed signs that Bane had been more than a coworker. "We'd like to see Dennis's office first."

"All right." The older man glanced at the receptionist. "Cara, is anyone out for a meeting this morning?"

"Not yet."

"You should be able to talk to everyone." He turned back to Robin and Nate, motioning for them to follow him. "This way to Dennis's office."

Accompanying the older man down a hallway carpeted in dusky green, they passed three offices before Eastman stopped in an open doorway. "Here we are."

The office was large, with a window that looked south. Green pressboard files were strewn across a credenza behind the heavy walnut desk. A photograph of Sheila Bane, and another of Dennis and Sheila together sat at one corner. Thick manuals stamped with city code numbers lined the shelves of one six-foot bookcase on an adjacent wall. In front of the desk sat two visitors' chairs in the same dark green leather as those in the waiting area.

Mr. Eastman stepped aside so Robin and Nate could enter. "Do you suspect foul play?"

"We're still sorting things out, sir." Nate moved to the far end of the desk occupied by a flat-screen monitor and laptop.

The other man looked at Nate. "The article in the paper said arson was a possible cause."

"We always have to eliminate a lot of possibilities before we know for sure."

Nate's answer was the same she would've given, Robin noted.

The company's owner nodded. "Well, if there's anything we can do, don't hesitate to ask."

"We'd like to take Mr. Bane's computer." Robin smiled. "We can get a warrant if you'd like."

"It's not necessary. Take it. All of us here will help in any way we can. It's so hard to believe Dennis is gone, and Sheila, too. Horrible tragedy to die that way."

Robin nodded.

"Would you like something to drink? Coffee? Cara brews a fresh pot every morning."

"No, thank you," Robin and Nate said in unison.

"I'll let you get to it, then. My office is straight down the hall. If you need anything at all, let me know."

"Thank you, sir." Once the man left, Nate moved behind the desk where Robin stood flipping through files. "Everyone seems cooperative."

"We'll know for sure when we start poking around

and asking questions." Catching Houston's subtle scent, she stepped away.

A thorough search of Bane's office turned up nothing helpful. Maybe his computer would. Carrying the laptop, Nate followed Robin out the door.

In addition to the receptionist and Mr. Eastman, there were ten leasing agents and four secretaries. Nate and Robin took turns questioning all of them, and one notable piece of information came to light.

Three different employees revealed that one of the secretaries, Tiffany Jarvis, had been openly pursuing Dennis Bane. Propositioning him, leaving notes on his desk, sending e-mails. According to all three people, Bane hadn't been interested at all and would barely pay attention to her.

Robin and Nate made their way to her desk, which sat outside the large offices of two leasing agents.

When they introduced themselves, she stood. Brown hair streaked with gold highlights fell to her shoulders. Her bloodshot hazel eyes were emphasized by thick mascara and eye shadow. She was dressed professionally, in a slim lilac skirt and coordinating floral sweater.

"Would you like to go into the break room or conference room, Miss Jarvis?" Nate asked.

She flicked a worried glance between him and Robin. "For privacy?"

Robin nodded, flipping to a blank page in her small notebook.

Leaving her desk, Tiffany started down a corridor. "We can go to the break room."

Once they got into the room outfitted with a long table, some chairs and a refrigerator, Robin didn't see any reason to beat around the bush. "We understand from a few of your coworkers that you were interested in Mr. Bane."

She hesitated. "It never went anywhere."

"Because he threatened to report your behavior to the police?"

The woman folded her arms around her middle. "He never would've done that. He was too nice. Besides, it wasn't like I was stalking him or anything."

"So the threat was just his way of getting you to back off?" Nate asked.

She nodded, shifting restlessly from one foot to the other.

Robin exchanged a look with Nate before continuing. "We were told you followed Mr. Bane to lunch sometimes, and out to the parking lot."

Her lips tightened. "Who told you that?"

"Yes or no, Miss Jarvis?" Robin asked.

The woman didn't answer.

"So, yes," Robin murmured.

Irritation flickered across Tiffany's face, but she didn't deny it.

Nate glanced over Robin's shoulder at her notes, his breath tickling her temple. "A few times you asked for a ride to or from work when there was nothing wrong with your car."

"That's just people talking." She looked anxiously past them into the hall. "I really need to get back to work."

Nate stood so close that Robin could feel the warmth of his body. She edged away, putting some space between her and the man who she was noticing way too much about. "We can finish this at Presley's police department."

"No, no. We can talk here."

"Good." She smiled. "Did you ever follow Dennis home?"

Tiffany stiffened. "No."

"You followed him other places," Nate pointed out.

She wouldn't meet his gaze. "Well, not there."

Judging from the flat look on Nate's face, he didn't believe the secretary any more than Robin did. "Where were you last Thursday night, Tiffany?"

"Is that the night it happened?"

"Yes." Nate looked at her expectantly. When she didn't respond, he prodded, "Miss Jarvis?"

"I was at a bar." She named a well-known spot.

Robin jotted a note. "Can anyone verify that?"

Her gaze flitted around the small room. "Is this going to take much longer?"

Nate's voice turned flinty. "Not if you answer the questions."

"I went alone and I left alone. Maybe the bartender will remember me." The woman tightened her arms around her middle. "Am I a suspect?"

"Thanks, Miss Jarvis." Robin tucked her notebook into the pocket of her slacks. "We'll get back to you if we have more questions."

"All right," Tiffany said shakily.

Finished for now, Robin and Nate stopped by Mr. Eastman's office to let him know they were leaving and taking Bane's computer. They both gave him their business cards, urging the older man to call if he or any of his employees thought of anything else.

Once outside the office, Robin and Nate boarded the elevator, Nate holding the laptop. Just before the doors closed, a group of people piled on. Eight of them. Nate eased back into the corner and Robin shifted, ignoring the flutter in her stomach. There was the usual shuffling and arranging, nudging for space. Just when she thought they were ready to go, another person jumped on. The doors closed and the car began to move.

All the maneuvering had landed Robin against the glass wall. And Nate. As the car started down, she felt a hard tug in her belly. The people who had joined them talked amongst themselves. Someone stepped on her foot and she edged away, pressing one hand against the solid side wall.

Standing close enough to brush Nate's torso with her shoulder, she determinedly kept her gaze fixed on the floor; but from the corner of her eye, she could see the levels as they zipped past. Even though she squeezed her eyes shut, it was too late.

The air turned stifling, and a giddy sensation clutched at her stomach. A cold sweat popped out on her nape. Woozy now, black spots danced behind her eyes. The *whoosh* of the car, the murmur of voices faded.

Breathe in, breathe out. Focusing helped, but she felt her control slipping. It wasn't the enclosed space that bothered her. It was the glass elevator. In the two seconds before she closed her eyes, she had seen enough to make her feel as though she were swept up in a circling funnel.

Crap! The world spun around her. Nate said something to her, but the words were thick, distorted. Part of her mind worked enough for her to grab the wall, which she did with her right hand, holding tight. The elevator shimmied to a stop and the spinning slowed.

Thank goodness they had stopped. Robin kept breathing steadily. The doors opened and people stepped off. She became aware then of a big hand cupping her elbow. Nate. And she had a death grip on his thigh. She hadn't been holding on to the wall at all. She'd grabbed Houston.

Heat from embarrassment and irritation flushed her body. She wanted to disappear through the floor. Swallowing a groan, she tried to pull away, but Nate held firm to her arm.

Which was good, she admitted to herself reluctantly, as her surroundings melded into a spinning top of glass, steel and the sky visible through the top of the building. She wobbled.

Once outside the elevator, he steered her to one of the padded chairs in the sitting area.

"Sit."

"I'll be fine."

"Sit," he said in a steely tone, one big hand on her shoulder, firmly pushing her into the seat. "What just happened in there? Did you almost pass out?"

"No!" Instead of sounding indignant, she sounded breathless. Shaken. *Aaargh!* Now that she was on a stationary surface, she sat unmoving, waiting for the whirling to stop. Her gaze went to Nate's thighs and the wrinkled fabric high on his leg.

"Your pants are wrinkled," she mumbled. "I'm sorry I grabbed hold of you in there."

"They're fine. I'll probably have a bruise on my leg, though," he teased, kneeling beside her. "You've got some grip."

"Oh, please."

"I thought you were trying to get a piece of me."

Her gaze shot to his before she realized he had said it so she would look at him. The warm concern in his face had her squirming. And her world began to right itself.

She started to stand, but he held her in place with a

hand on her leg. His gaze scoured her face. "Tell me what's going on. Do you have some sort of condition? When we're together, should I be on medical alert?"

"You're adorable," she said with a withering look. Her entire body burned with embarrassment. "No."

"Well?"

"It's not a big deal."

"Daly," he growled.

She hated this. *Hated* it. Hated the loss of control, the sense of moving when she wasn't, of being off-balance. "I don't handle those kinds of elevators well."

"No, really?" His wry tone said he had already figured that out. "You didn't seem to have any trouble on the way up."

That was because she had been able to focus on the solid doors.

"Do you have a fear of heights?"

"Not fear, no, but they don't like me."

"Then what is it?"

"Vertigo. Most elevators don't bother me, but glass ones do. As you saw."

"Would you have fallen? Passed out?"

"I wouldn't have passed out," she dismissed with a short laugh. Falling, though, was a real possibility. "The most I've ever done is slide to the floor in a puddle. You should've seen my first time on a Ferris wheel before I knew I had it."

"We could have gotten off."

"The damage was already done, and my brain wasn't working too well."

"If I'd known, I could've gotten you to the front of the elevator." His breathed teased her hair.

No way would she have told him she needed to do that. "That's all right. I'm fine."

"No, you aren't. You should've told me."

She looked away. "I don't like this thing to dictate my life."

"One day is hardly your—"

"Look, I'm already better." And she was. Enough so that she wanted to bury her face in his neck and breathe in his clean male scent. The urge spurred a burst of panic. "I didn't pass out or scream bloody murder or get sick."

"Well, you scared the hell out of me."

The husky tone of his voice had her gaze locking on his. "Oh, come on."

"You should've told me about it."

"It doesn't happen that often."

"Just when you're in elevators," he said pointedly.

"Glass elevators," she corrected. Or really high, open spaces. "As long as I don't look down, I'm okay."

"Does McClain know about this?"

She nodded.

Watching her steadily, Nate grazed a finger down her temple, moving back a damp strand of hair.

His light touch had her pulse hitching. She had an insane urge to grab his hand and hold tight. Instead, she reached up and tucked her hair back into her French braid, struggling to pull her gaze from his. She got to her feet. This time he let her.

"I'm good to go."

Even though he looked doubtful, he stepped back and picked up the computer from the chair beside hers, walking with her to the door.

The sense of motion had stopped, but she still felt off-balance. This time, it was because of the big man who stood so close to her. She didn't like that.

Once outside, the heat engulfed them. The *vroom* of

traffic sounded on the nearby highway, and her nose twitched at the smell of car fuel.

Still mortified, she could barely look at Nate. The last thing she needed was for the man overseeing the task force, *the man who was her temporary boss,* to think she had a problem. Especially one brought on by something as innocuous as riding in an elevator!

And if that weren't bad enough, her heart rate had gone haywire just because he touched her face. That made her feel ridiculous. And hyped up.

Work. She needed to think about work.

Getting back on track, her gaze flicked to him. "I think Miss Jarvis is lying about being in Bane's neighborhood. She followed him everywhere else. Why not home?"

"I agree. Plus it was at that point in the interview when she started to get jumpy. Maybe Bane's computer will give us something."

Robin nodded. "When we get back to the P.D., we can run her through the system, to see if anything comes up."

The sun beat down on them and Nate thumbed a bead of sweat from his temple. Her gaze skimmed over the bronze column of his neck and across his hard, wide shoulders, down his muscular arms to his hands. Large strong hands. Gentle hands.

She and Nate had been all business until she did her impression of a drunk and he had helped her. Touched her. His finger against her skin had been soft, yet it pulled at some invisible wire inside her, drew her closer to him. Was *still* drawing her. There had been nothing businesslike about that at all.

As they reached his SUV, he unlocked the doors

with his remote. "I told McClain we would update him sometime today."

"Let's wait and see if we get anything on Tiffany."

"All right." He opened her door.

She started to slide in, then paused. She didn't want what had happened in the elevator to get around, but she was at his mercy. "Um, Houston, you don't need to tell anyone about…that."

"'That'?"

She fluttered a hand in the direction of the tower. *That.*

Concern flashed through his eyes. *No, no,* Robin thought, *please don't make a big deal out of this.*

Then a grin hitched up one corner of his mouth. "What's it worth to you for me to keep quiet?"

Relief swept through her and she gave him a mock glare. "Are you forgetting I carry a gun?"

He chuckled and closed her door, jogging around to the driver's side and climbing in. "Your secret's safe with me. Scout's honor."

Just as she started to thank him for being so nice, she was hit with a sudden suspicion. "Were you ever even a Boy Scout?"

His blue eyes twinkled at her. "No."

That drew a surprised laugh from her. As he joined in, she admitted what she had been fighting since Saturday. Dammit, she did like the guy.

Nate was learning all kinds of things about Robin. On Saturday at the softball game, he had noticed a long, jagged scar on her right leg, between her ankle and calf. And today he found out she had vertigo.

Her startling reaction on the elevator had caused his heart to clench hard as she had clamped on to his leg.

If he had needed a big red flag that something was wrong, that was it. No way would she have touched him voluntarily.

An hour later at the police department, he was still thinking about that, as well as the naked vulnerability in her waxy face when he had steered her out of the elevator. Her unguarded expression had reminded him of the day of her wedding. That time, the stormy emotion in her eyes had been pain caused by the bombshell of learning she had been left at the altar. Today, the look in her eyes had been just as raw.

For the first time since Nate had begun working with her, he saw Robin as more woman than cop. And he liked it.

As they walked into the large, dingy room of the homicide division, he was glad she had color back in her face. A tightness in his chest eased. Despite teasing her, he wouldn't have told anyone about her vertigo, unless his keeping quiet would have put her or her partner in danger. McClain already knew, so Nate saw no reason why anyone else needed to.

He stood behind her chair at her metal desk as she ran Tiffany Jarvis through the police database, but his attention wasn't on the woman they had just interviewed. It was on Robin. He could touch her just by lifting a finger.

It would take only one movement to stroke the toned, golden-tan arm, bared by a sleeveless top. Or the tender patch of skin behind her ear. Or the silky hair she had pulled into a sleek twist.

The two of them had been getting along. She may not have forgiven him for the part he had played in scrapping her wedding, but she didn't still seem to be holding a grudge. Things between them had been easy, professional—until her vertigo had struck.

Robin shifted in her chair, looking up at him. "Tiffany Jarvis isn't in the system. She doesn't have so much as a traffic ticket."

"I still think she's lying about never having followed Bane home."

"Same here."

"Is there somewhere else we can look?" Nate stepped back so Robin could stand. When she did, he caught a whiff of her wild-flower scent.

"Just because she isn't in the system," she said, "doesn't mean she wasn't ever seen near Bane's house."

"So we go back and talk to the neighbors again?"

"Yes." Robin stepped around her desk and started for the door. "And let's stop by the traffic division. Maybe the officer assigned to that area saw her."

Nate followed her past the rows of putty-colored desks and out to the hall. His gaze slid over her slender curves. The dusky blue vest and matching slacks skimmed over a small waist, the gentle flare of her hips.

The disappointment that had shot through him earlier when he'd seen her fantastic legs were covered by slacks had disappeared. She looked damn fine in what she wore today, too. His gaze lingered on her backside. He wouldn't mind getting his hands on her there, either.

He had to admit he was doing more than his share of looking. Since the ballgame on Saturday, he had also done more than his share of thinking about her, and only one of those times had involved the investigation.

There wasn't any getting around it now. He wanted to know about her, wanted to know what she thought about things. He just plain wanted her. No way in hell could he let on. She would run so fast she would leave skid marks up his back.

They walked into a large room that was nearly identical to the one where the homicide detectives worked. Same gray-speckled floor, same sturdy desks, same battered file cabinets. And at the far wall sat Kyle Emrick, Robin's former fiancé. A sudden tension lashed the air when the man lifted a hand in greeting.

Nate nodded, shifting his attention back to Robin.

She spoke to a young officer, asking the name of the patrolman assigned to the area where Bane and his wife had resided.

Emrick started toward him. "Houston, I heard you'd moved back."

"Hi." Nate shook the other man's hand. The strain became more pronounced when Robin straightened and looked at her ex, an unreadable expression on her face. Nate wondered how this meeting would go.

If he had been in her position, Nate couldn't have said how he would act.

"I understand Fuller Street is on your beat," she said to Emrick.

"Yeah."

She held out the sheet of information they had gotten on Tiffany Jarvis. Among other things, it listed the woman's full name, address, date of birth, and the make and model of the car she drove, as well as identifying marks. "We need to know if you recognize this woman's name or have seen this car before."

Just at six feet tall and runner-lean, the other man stroked the goatee he had grown since Nate had last seen him. "Oh, a late model red Thunderbird with a dented left fender. Yes, I've seen it before, on Fuller."

Robin shared a look with Nate. "Did you see it more than once?"

"Yes, and recently I saw it two times within a short period of time."

Emrick returned the sheet of paper to her.

Her voice and demeanor were calm, composed. She might appear to be engaging in conversation with her ex, but Nate could tell she was looking right through the guy. He didn't know if she had been forced to deal with Emrick at work before. Regardless, she seemed to have come to grips with the past.

"Do you remember exactly when you saw the car?" she asked. "A week ago? A month ago?"

"Last week." He paused thoughtfully. "Once on Wednesday after dark, and again on Thursday about the same time."

Adrenaline shot through Nate as he glanced at Robin.

She pressed the other man. "Thursday. How can you be sure of the day?"

"The cable company hit a water line when they were digging and the block was closed so the city trucks could get in and fix it. I had to ask her to move her car."

"What block of Fuller?"

"Eight hundred."

Bingo, Nate thought. *Right on Bane's street.*

Robin exchanged a look with Nate, the glint in her eye telling him she was as excited as he was about catching Tiffany Jarvis in at least one lie.

It didn't prove the secretary was the Mailman, or had even been the one to set the blaze, but if they had caught her in one lie, they might catch her in another. Now they needed to see if they could connect her to either of the other fires or victims.

"Is this about the fire-murders on Fuller Street last week?" At Nate's nod, Emrick eyed Nate and Robin curiously. "You two working together?"

"Yes," Nate said.

Emrick's gaze trailed slowly over Robin. "I thought you were working that case and another with Collier McClain."

"I am," she said flatly, offering nothing further.

Her ex's features tightened and Nate thought he saw regret in the other man's dark eyes. Had Kyle finally realized what a stupid mistake he had made by ruining his relationship with Robin?

Nate followed up on Emrick's observation. "The powers that be formed a task force. We're both assigned there, and so is McClain."

Robin's face remained blank.

Nate hadn't made it a point to keep in touch with Emrick over the years, but they had talked occasionally. At least two of those times, Kyle had sworn that he had explained to Robin why he had left her at the altar and why Nate had gotten involved.

But watching the two of them now, he didn't buy it. He caught another hot look Emrick slid down Robin's body. And the snap of antagonism in her stance.

The other man still wanted her. She was definitely not interested, which served him right, after what he had done to her.

Emrick stepped toward her. "If I think of anything else I'll let you know."

She nodded, shifting her gaze to the officer she had first spoken to. "Thanks for the help, both of you."

She strode out of the room without a backward glance. She seemed to have gotten past the mess with Emrick and was handling it well.

When Nate caught up to her, she smiled, excitement sparkling in her eyes. "Well, that confirms Tiffany was lying about at least one thing."

"Do you want to go back and talk to her right now?"

"Yes. Plus we can ask around in Bane's neighborhood and find out if anyone else saw her car."

As they stopped at Robin's desk so she could get her purse, Nate couldn't stem his curiosity about her interaction with her ex. "Do you have to see him very often?"

"Him? Oh, Kyle? Not really. I try to stay away from him."

"Makes sense," Nate murmured. "He's a jackass."

"He's more ass than jack, but that's just my opinion," she said with false sweetness.

Nate grinned. She would get no argument from him. The last time he had spoken to Emrick had been when the man had called to ask Nate to be a groomsman in his second wedding. Nate had declined.

One reason was because he wanted nothing to do with another "Emrick Special." And the other was because, at that time, it had been only a year since Nate's divorce, and he wanted no part of *any* wedding.

Nate realized he was thinking more about Robin than about the woman who may have just become their primary suspect. "I heard Emrick was getting a divorce."

Robin's gaze rose slowly to his, her blue eyes glittering. "I heard that, too."

"How long was he married? Was it even two years?"

"About that, I think." She angled her jaw at him, no sign of wobbliness now.

He couldn't help following the graceful line of her neck, the pulse throbbing in the hollow of her throat. He thought about his mouth doing the same thing.

"What's the deal, Houston?" she demanded. "You think I should thank you for 'saving me' from the jerk?"

"No. I was just curious."

She huffed out a breath and moved past him, headed for the squad room door. "I bet his wife has no idea why he's leaving her, and she probably won't get any more information than I did."

"Which was what?" He followed, trying to keep his voice casual, but the suspicion he had felt earlier bored deep.

"Nada, zero," she said. "Zip."

Shock drummed through him. "Nothing at all?"

"Nothing."

"Have you asked him recently?"

"You're kidding, right?" She gave him a blistering look over her shoulder. "During the year after everything fell apart, I asked plenty. He just kept blaming *you*. And while your butting in still makes me mad, in the end he was the one who made the choice to walk away. I'd still like to know why he weaseled out, but not badly enough to drag everything back up. That's something I have no desire to relive. It was hard enough the first time."

As Nate came up beside her, her eyes turned to hard blue glass. "I'm sure you can understand if I'm not wild about talking to *you* about it, either."

Ouch. Yes, Nate understood. And he also understood that instead of coming over to say hello, Kyle had really come over to determine whether Nate had told Robin the truth about calling off the ceremony.

Anger and disbelief flared inside him. Kyle hadn't

explained to Robin why he had left her at the altar, hadn't told her anything about sleeping with her sister in the small office at the church.

That lying SOB hadn't told her *anything*.

She still had no idea why Nate had interfered in her wedding.

Chapter 5

Three hours later, Nate was still thinking about the fact that Emrick had told Robin nothing about why he had called off their wedding. Neither had Robin's sister. Neither had Nate.

He should tell her. Shouldn't he?

The whole time he and Robin had reinterviewed Bane's neighbors, Nate thought about it. If it had been his place to tell her, he would have already done it. But it wasn't his place. Until he had started working with Robin, he had barely known the woman, had seen her a total of two times, both at her wedding.

Robin's being in the dark as to why Nate had convinced Kyle to walk away was just one thing Nate was still trying to process. The hot, hungry look Emrick had run over Robin's body had wound something tight inside Nate. A need to protect that had taken him completely off guard. He wasn't sure what to do with that. Daly carried a gun, for crying out loud. She didn't need his protection.

When an older woman in Bane's neighborhood confirmed seeing a red T-bird and the woman driver, who matched the description given of Tiffany Jarvis, Nate and Robin had what they needed to question the secretary further.

En route to the woman's office, they stopped at Presley's police department to pick up the e-mails and photos printed from Dennis Bane's laptop. The tech wasn't finished examining the computer, but Nate and Robin planned to go through what was available so far on their way downtown.

Since their conversation about her ex, Robin had been quiet. Now, as she and Nate strode down the dimly lit hallway toward the homicide room, she slid him a sideways look. "I can pick up Tiffany on my own, if you have other things you need to handle."

The cool remoteness of her tone had him wondering if she was trying to get rid of him. She didn't seem irritated, which she had plainly been when he had asked about communication between her and Emrick, but what did Nate know? "This is what I need to be doing. It's my case, too."

"Right."

He could read nothing in her blank expression. Following her into the squad room, he nearly ran into her when she stopped short.

"Beau Tyler!" she exclaimed.

A big man in an Oklahoma City police uniform bent over her desk, writing a note. As he straightened, a grin stretched across his face. "Hey, Detective."

"Knock it off." She quickly reached the sandy-haired

man who was a couple of inches taller than Nate's six foot three.

Tyler bent down to meet her hug. She pulled back, looking him up and down. "How are you?"

"Great." He glanced over her head and Robin turned, following his gaze. There was a warmth in her eyes that had never been there when she looked at Nate. She gestured to him. "Beau, this is Agent Houston with the fire marshal's office. We're working some cases together."

"Nice to meet you."

Nate nodded, shaking the man's hand.

The other man hitched a thumb toward Robin. "I guess you've figured out by now, this one will keep you in line."

She chuckled and Nate studied her face. This was the first time he had seen her so open with anyone. What was her relationship with the younger man? Though there was no mistaking the adoration on Tyler's face, it seemed born more of respect than desire. Like brother and sister.

Beau grinned, dark eyes twinkling. "If Robin hadn't straightened me out, I'd probably be doing a stretch at McAlester."

"Oh, you would not."

"When I was fifteen," he went on, "she arrested me for trying to steal a car."

Sliding his hands into the pockets of his slacks, Nate listened as Robin and Beau asked about each other's families. His gaze did a slow hike up her slender figure, and an odd tightness settled in his chest. She was slight, seemed even more delicate next to the friend who towered above her.

Her curvy, petite frame was deceptive. After the

vertigo episode, he'd seen a raw vulnerability in her, but there was a core of strength there, too. It would be hard for her to hear that the woman Nate had caught with her ex-fiancé was her sister, but his gut said she could handle it.

Still, it wasn't his place to tell. Not then, not now. That information should come from Kyle or her sister. Seeing as how five years had passed without either of them confessing, Nate didn't see that happening.

He clicked back into her conversation with Beau, who said "I have a reason for coming by."

"You know you don't need one."

The affection on her face lit her up from the inside and Nate couldn't tear his gaze away. Her sun-kissed skin glowed. He found his attention on the curve of her pale, pink lips.

Tyler eased down onto the edge of her desk. "I wanted to let you know I was accepted to the FBI Academy."

"You're going to Quantico to train as a special agent!"

He chuckled. "Can you believe it?"

"Absolutely." She hugged him again. "When do you go?"

"In a month."

"Congratulations. I knew you could do it."

"Thanks to you," he said earnestly.

"You did the work."

"You gave me a chance, and I appreciate it." Before she could respond, he said, "And now the other reason I came. Lauren and I are getting married in two weeks."

She glanced down as he handed her an invitation. "It's about time she made an honest man of you!"

"That's what I told her," he said with a grin. "I know

you're not big on weddings, but it would mean a lot to us if you came."

"Of course I will. I may not want a wedding, but I don't mind other people having them."

Her view on marriage was the same as Nate's. Not hard to understand why, in her case. Tyler had obviously heard about her being left at the altar, could've been there that day for all Nate knew.

Beau got to his feet and bent to hug Robin again. "I have to get out of here."

"All right. I'm so glad you stopped by."

He started out the door, saying to Nate, "Nice to meet you."

"You, too."

"Two weeks, Robin," Beau reminded.

"I'll be there." After the man disappeared, she studied the invitation with a smile.

"You mentored him?" Nate asked. "Seems like a good guy."

"He is." She sobered, looking thoughtful. "Maybe if I'd given my sister as much attention as I did Beau, things would be different between us."

"Wendy, right?" Not that he was likely to forget her sister's name.

Robin's gaze shot to his, as though she hadn't meant to say that out loud.

"At your wedding, wasn't she engaged?"

"Yes." She carefully placed the invitation in the middle drawer of her desk. "That didn't work out."

"Are you guys close?"

"Not really. We never have been," she said matter-of-factly. "Are you close with your sister?"

"Yeah. Becca's always been there for me, especially when we were kids." He thought about the hellacious years he and his sister had weathered during and after their parents' bitter divorce. "She put me first too many times to count."

"That's really nice. My relationship with Wendy has never been like that."

"Why not?"

"We just never seemed to click." She frowned thoughtfully. "She always wanted what I had, even after we were adults. Clothes, shoes."

Fiancé, Nate thought.

She waved a dismissive hand. "It's not like we hate each other. There just has never been much to our relationship."

And if he told Robin what part Wendy had played in ruining her wedding, there would be even less to it.

She picked up the folder left by the computer tech, walking out the door with Nate. "You want to drive while I look through these e-mails?"

"Sure." Reaching over her head, he pushed open the front glass door of the P.D. and waited for her to precede him outside.

As she passed, his gaze traced the graceful line of her spine, rested on the sweet curve of her backside for a moment.

She seemed to have reached a place where her head wasn't stuck in the past. He remembered all too well how long it had taken him to get to that point after his divorce. Finding out about her sister would only cause Robin pain, and he didn't want that.

There was that urge to protect again. Not telling her made him feel guilty, but this wasn't about him. He forced himself to examine his reasons for wanting to tell her about Kyle and Wendy. Did he want her to know the truth about her aborted wedding because he thought she had a right to know? Or because he wanted to clear his conscience? Or even because he hadn't liked the too-interested look Emrick had given Robin earlier and he wanted the man away from her?

Nate dragged a hand across his nape. Telling her the truth would change nothing. It *would* cause her more pain, especially regarding her sister.

He still remembered the hurt in her eyes the day of the wedding, and he didn't want to see such anguish there again. He sure as hell didn't want to be the one who caused it.

Hadn't Emrick hurt her enough already? Hadn't Nate?

He couldn't tell her he had walked in on Kyle having sex with her sister. He wouldn't.

Nate was really doing a number on her, Robin admitted to herself, reluctantly. She hadn't liked talking to him about Kyle, mainly because she preferred to give the guy as little air time as possible, in her head or aloud. But also because she was starting not to want to think about Kyle and Nate in the same sentence.

Her emotions were churning, though not due to her ex-fiancé. No, this turmoil was caused by a keen, sharp-edged awareness of the hunky fire marshal currently working cases with her.

When he looked at her, her body went soft in ways—in places—she didn't appreciate. She hadn't been able to completely erase the feel of his hand on her arm, his touch on her face this morning.

With only feet separating them in his SUV, Robin breathed in his clean, spicy scent, as her gaze traveled over powerful thighs, the broad hand that palmed the steering wheel, the arms that were hard muscle and sinew. A little shiver worked through her. Okay, so her hormones were paying attention. That didn't mean she was going to do anything about it. She *wasn't* going to.

As they traveled south on Centennial Expressway, she opened the file folder of Bane's e-mails, a stack almost an inch thick. Nate called Eastman and Associates and asked for Tiffany.

After a brief exchange, he hung up. "She's out to lunch, should be back in an hour. Want to stop and get some lunch ourselves?"

"Sure, if we can go somewhere that serves relatively fast."

Before she could do more than note that the tech had sorted all the pictures together and laid them on top, Nate stopped at a small deli. Once back in his SUV, it only took a couple of minutes for Robin to flip through the printed photos that had been on Bane's computer.

"No pictures here of Tiffany or body parts that might be Tiffany's."

Nate grinned as he changed lanes. "You mean like naked, headless shots?"

"Yes." Sliding the pictures to the back of the batch, she skimmed several e-mails before she spotted Tiffany's name. "Ah, here's one from her. 'Dennis, I'm going to crawl under your desk and unzip your—'"

Robin slapped the paper facedown. "Okay, we get the gist."

A wicked grin tugged at Nate's lips. "It sounded like you were just getting to the good part."

Her face flamed as she gave him a look. "You can read that for yourself later, if you want."

She thumbed to the next message, which was just as

explicit. As was the next one and the next. "Good grief," Robin muttered.

"What did you find?"

"So far, nothing except sex stuff. Did this girl think about anything else? I've read five, and they're basically the same with a couple of…special things thrown in for variety. It looks as though there are more. Let's just say Tiffany had a plan for Dennis Bane."

"If she told the truth, and he really wasn't interested," Nate said, "he was probably already getting plenty somewhere else."

"Right."

Nate exited the highway and a few minutes later turned into the parking lot of the tower that housed Eastman and Associates. "Maybe Tiffany returned in the time it took us to get down here. I'll drive through the lot and see if I can spot her car."

"Good idea." Robin read message after message, her skin heating. All the stroking and licking and kissing going on in the explicit e-mails had her shifting uncomfortably on the seat.

She adjusted the closest air-conditioner vent in her direction to cool off. Ignoring the amused look Nate flicked her way, she continued to work her way through the stack. Finally, she came to a message that wasn't from the secretary who seemed to have fixated on Dennis Bane.

Relief shot through her. "Oh, good. Here are e-mails from other people, most about work projects and closings. One about the company picnic, another about a blood drive."

As Nate drove slowly through the lot, he again called Tiffany's office. "She isn't back yet. The receptionist volunteered that all their employees use the underground parking garage, so we might find her down there."

Robin nodded. "There are several emails from Bane's wife, Sheila."

Nate took the ramp into the underground parking garage, the light dimming considerably as they moved out of direct sunlight. Open sections around the garage saved the area from being dark, though Robin had to let her eyes adjust to the change from bright to shade. Being out of the sun's heat made the space cooler, but the air was still warm and heavy with humidity.

As Nate drove up and down the aisles, he checked the vehicles on one side while Robin scanned the other. The faint tang of car fuel hung in the air, as well as a mix of scents from nearby restaurants.

Neither of them spotted the red Thunderbird. Nate pointed to the end of their current row. "There's only one bank of elevators. If we park close, we'll be able to see her going inside, in case we miss her when she drives in."

He pulled into a nearby space, glancing at her. "I'm going to keep the truck running so we can have the AC. Want me to look at half of those?"

"I can just imagine which ones you want to look at," she said dryly.

He chuckled. "I'll take half of the ones you haven't read yet."

"Okay." She passed him a batch. "I wish we could find something from Dennis to Tiffany. So far, any correspondence between them has been from her to him."

For a moment, the only sounds in the car were the hum of the air conditioner, the faint sound of the radio and the occasional crinkle of paper.

Nate pulled out one of the messages. "I may have found something. This one is from Dennis to Tiffany. Short and to the point. 'Don't call my house or come by there again. I *will* call the cops.' It's dated about two weeks before the fire that killed him and his wife."

"So we know Tiffany was seen near his house at least twice in the weeks leading up to his death, after he had specifically told her to stay away." Pleased, she shifted toward him. "That's good, Houston. Really good."

"Want me to keep going?"

"Yes. Everything we find gives us more to ask about when we take her in for questioning."

They fell silent, both reading. They were separated only by a console. Now that they had stopped moving, Robin became absurdly conscious of the fact that they were alone. In a small, enclosed space. Enclosed enough that she could see the tic of his pulse in the hollow of his strong throat. Watch the subtle changes of his expression as he read.

The shadows did nothing to soften his solid jaw or hide his dimple. That killer dimple.

Her gaze went to his left hand. And bare ring finger. She remembered Meredith telling her that at the time of Robin's wedding, Nate had been trying to work things out with his wife. She wondered what had happened between them. It was really none of her business. Still, he hadn't minded quizzing *her*.

He already knew about the most humiliating experience of her life. Why shouldn't she ask questions, too?

"At my wedding, you were trying to work things out with your ex-wife. Weren't able to, I guess."

Without looking up from the sheaf of papers in his hand, he shook his head.

"Think you'll ever give marriage another shot?"

"No." No hesitation, no doubt in his voice.

Robin felt exactly the same way. "I know why I won't. What's your reason?"

A sudden tension vibrated in him, and his gaze shifted to hers. "Why do you want to know?"

"You know everything about my reasons." It might have been a trick of the light, but she thought he stiffened. "It seems only fair."

Apparently, he didn't like talking about it. Big surprise. Neither did she. Maybe from now on, he wouldn't ask any more questions about her wedding-that-wasn't.

She expected him to continue reading. Instead, he angled one shoulder into the corner against the door and draped a hand over the steering wheel. His eyes glittered like blue steel in the shadowy light.

"Just after our fourth anniversary, I found out my ex-wife was cheating on me."

"Yeow. I'm sorry." Robin's heart tugged hard. She wanted to take his hand or hug him. Comfort him. Something she didn't do with a lot of people. The unfamiliar impulse had to be caused by her crazy attraction to him.

"When my sister and I were kids, our parents split up. It got ugly fast and stayed that way for a few years. I swore if I ever got married I wouldn't get a divorce. Put anyone, including me, through that kind of hell."

The rich baritone of his voice set off a ripple of sensation under her skin. Robin found herself leaning closer.

"I was willing to do whatever it took to keep my marriage together. My ex said she was, too. We saw a counselor for two years, until I realized I was doing all the heavy lifting and she was drifting farther away." He dragged a hand down his face, a terse edge in his words. "So, after six years, we called it quits, and that's how I bombed out at my one and only try. Not going back there again."

For a second, she glimpsed a grimness in his eyes that she had seen mirrored in her own. Memories of the past. "Thanks for telling me. I admire you for trying to work it out. A lot of people wouldn't have."

Without thinking, she reached out to lay a hand on his thigh. His gaze dropped. The air between them turned hot, pulsing. His hand covered hers and he rubbed his thumb across her knuckles.

Robin stared down at the bronze of his skin next to the creamy rose of hers. An ache bloomed deep inside her.

She told herself to pull back. The command sounded loud and clear from her brain, yet her body didn't move.

His eyes darkened. A current of electricity snapped tight between them. He shifted closer and she knew by the hunger in his face he was going to kiss her. There were all kinds of reasons why she shouldn't let him do it. Right now, she couldn't think of a single one.

This was crazy. Borderline stupid. Since her bout with vertigo, Nate had watched her with a quiet intensity that stirred something inside her. Something she felt unable to control.

So when he tugged her toward him, she went. She wanted to know what his kiss would be like, how he tasted.

She felt helpless to resist. The barely there brush of his lips hollowed out her belly. When she didn't pull away, his mouth fully covered hers.

She sank into the kiss, silky and deep and hot. The only places they had contact were their hands and lips, yet she felt his touch on every burning inch of her body. His kiss wasn't tentative, but it was slow. Exploring. Demanding.

When she opened her mouth under his, he stroked her tongue and took the kiss deeper. She was dimly aware of her hand tightening on his rock-hard thigh, of his hand on her nape, holding her to him. His clean, sharp, male scent filled her head. The inside of his mouth was cool from the iced tea he had brought with him from the deli. She began to shake.

Wanting to completely surrender, it took a few seconds for her brain to engage. It finally did.

How could she feel this overwhelming desire for the man who had caused the most humiliating experience of her life? What was wrong with her?

The effort required to pull away surprised her. She was breathing hard, as was he. When she managed to open her eyes, she saw the flush of arousal across his cheekbones and smoldering in his blue eyes.

She felt it, too. Hammering through her with every beat of her heart.

She flattened her hand against his chest, hard and hot beneath her touch. Her head was spinning, and not because of her vertigo.

"Whoa," she said huskily, to herself as much as to him. "Just…*whoa*."

He grazed his thumb lightly against the corner of her mouth, setting off another flurry of sensation in her belly. And a burst of panic.

She eased away. "That wasn't a good idea."

"Felt pretty good to me."

The low, raspy words stroked over her. She gave him a dark look. "I'm not kidding, Houston."

"Neither am I."

The way he looked at her, *into* her, with those piercing eyes made her want to dive right back in for another kiss.

Searching for a way out, Robin nearly wilted with relief when she saw Tiffany Jarvis approaching the building's elevators. "There she is."

After a long, steady look, Nate followed her gaze. A muscle flexed in his jaw.

"Let's go." Still struggling to regain her mental balance, Robin got out and met him at the hood of the vehicle.

They walked toward the secretary, who was accompanied by two other women. Robin recognized them from the earlier interview at Eastman's office.

Now that she had put some space between her and Nate, she could breathe. Think.

She had just kissed the man who had shattered her world. And she wanted to do it again! What was wrong with her?

Whenever she was around him, her unshakeable control seemed to disintegrate. This wild, unrestrained feeling scared the hell out of her.

Nate Houston scared the hell out of her.

She had let her guard down. She couldn't do it again.

Chapter 6

Thirty minutes later, Robin and Nate stood in an interview room at the police department, questioning Tiffany Jarvis. She had agreed to talk to them while waiting for her attorney, and now sat in a metal chair, at a scratched, rectangular table in the center of the room. Another metal chair stood in the far corner.

Robin's nerves were still fluttering from that kiss. There was no denying it had turned her to liquid, but she had a job to do. It helped that Nate had finally stopped eyeing her with a mix of heated curiosity and frustration.

Well, she was frustrated, too. Yet, she forced herself to focus on the woman they were interviewing, not on Nate or kissing Nate or what he had told her about his ex-wife and parents.

She hadn't gone through anything nearly as brutal as

what had happened to break up his marriage, but Robin felt a connection to him anyway.

The thought had tension coiling inside her. It was hard enough to wrap her mind around the fact that she liked him, let alone admit she felt connected to him. And wanted him. Even knowing she should keep up her guard, she had let him get to her. In a big way.

She had thought she was in control. Yeah, she'd controlled herself, all right. Practically into his lap. She bit back a groan and repeated the question she had just asked. "Again, Ms. Jarvis, were you ever in Dennis Bane's house?"

The woman gave her a mulish look, sitting back in her chair and folding her arms. Robin exchanged a look with Nate.

He stood a few feet away, one shoulder braced against the wall in a deceptively relaxed pose. "If we find your prints, things will only look worse for you. You might as well tell us. The truth, this time."

Robin flattened her hands on the table's surface, leaning toward Tiffany. "A Presley patrol cop identified your car in Bane's neighborhood on two separate occasions."

The other woman's gaze flickered to Robin then away.

She opened the file folder filled with the printouts from Bane's computer. "We also found several e-mails from you to Dennis. Sexually explicit e-mails."

"And one from him to you." Nate pushed away from the wall and walked over, thumping the piece of paper on top of the stack. "Telling you to stop calling his house and coming by there. Which means you called his house *and* went there at least once. You told us you'd never been. Why did you lie?"

"Because I didn't think you'd believe me!" she burst out.

"Knowing you've already lied doesn't make us inclined to do that," Robin pointed out.

"Help yourself," Nate urged. "No more lies."

"I was in his house for a work party. And only once."

"So you would've known how to get back in, where to plant the accelerant."

Robin flicked a glance at Nate, liking that he kept pushing.

"Plant accelerant?" The secretary looked startled. "Wasn't this fire an accident? I mean, I know the paper said it might have been arson, but—"

"It was arson," Nate said flatly.

"Murder," Robin added, watching Tiffany's face carefully.

The other woman drew in a sharp breath. "I would never kill anyone, and I don't know anything about accelerants."

Nate arched a brow and Robin figured he was thinking the same thing she was. They couldn't prove Tiffany had planted anything, but if they obtained a search warrant for her house, they might find number-ten envelopes, chlorine powder and petroleum jelly, like what had been used.

"These e-mails, the cop's ID and your admission of being in Bane's house are enough to get us a warrant to search your house."

At Robin's words, the other woman's jaw set.

Nate leveled a look on Tiffany. "The cop who identified you said he saw you on Bane's street the night before the fire and the night of the fire."

"I told you I was at a bar at the time that fire started!"

"That's the beauty of this accelerant," Nate said. "You could've been far away by the time it ignited."

"I didn't do it."

Robin shrugged. "The bartender didn't remember you."

"Well, I was there."

A knock sounded on the door and Captain Hager stepped inside with a sharp-faced, perfectly groomed man. Robin was already groaning inwardly when her boss said, "Ms. Jarvis's attorney, Mr. Meacham, is here."

Yippee. With his meticulously arranged hair and bottle tan, Robin thought the blond lawyer looked like a Ken doll.

Shrewd, dark eyes met hers. "Detective, this interview is over."

"We'll have more questions later," she said coolly, frustrated they hadn't gotten further.

The attorney took Tiffany's arm and steered her outside the room, passing Robin a business card. "Any more questions should go through me."

She slid the card into her slacks pocket, making a sound low in her throat as Meacham disappeared with his client.

Nate went to the door, watching the departing pair. He dragged a hand across his nape. "Do you believe her about being in Bane's house only once?"

"No, but we can't prove it. We'll get a warrant and see if we can find anything at her place."

"We need to try and connect her to the other fire-murders, too."

"Go back over the files, interviews, all of it."

He nodded.

While questioning Tiffany, Robin's mind had been occupied with something besides memories of that kiss, but now she found herself staring at Nate's mouth. Remembering… There was still a faint tingle in her blood. She didn't understand it; she had never been this affected by a man, not even Kyle.

She jerked her gaze away. "It's hard to believe someone like Jarvis would know that much about accelerants, especially this one. I mean, it's not elementary, like pouring gas and throwing a match on it. Could she learn on the Internet about something like that?"

"I'd like to say no, but all kinds of information is on there, and the items used by the Mailman aren't difficult to get."

"Does anything about what we've learned concerning Tiffany remind you of the serial fire setter you put away in Chicago? Like being fixated on someone at work? Being in the victims' homes for at least one social occasion? Anything?"

"No."

"So maybe you didn't make a mistake."

His eyes widened.

A little surprised at herself for saying it, Robin gave him a small smile. For the first time, she admitted it was possible he hadn't made a mistake about her wedding, either. Their gazes met and Robin felt that connection again, the one she had felt earlier in the parking garage.

The silence grew taut and after a moment he cleared his throat. "If Tiffany is our torch, we may have to rethink our theory about the twenty-seven-day cooling-off period being due to the Mailman's job. Jobs such as hers don't operate in shifts like the ones we've checked into so far. There would be another reason for the number of days in between fire-murders."

"True." Robin closed the file folder, glancing up to find his attention on her lips.

Her pulse hitched, then went crazy when his gaze did a slow hike down her body. Awareness vibrated in every cell in her body, and in a flash she again felt the searing slide of his mouth on hers.

The steady look on his face had Robin wondering if he knew what she was thinking. Just as she started to tell him to knock it off, he asked, "Are we going to talk about the kiss?"

"Shh!" Even though she knew they were alone, she glanced around the room. "No."

"Why not?"

"I'm not interested in talking about it."

"What if I am?"

His husky words had her swallowing hard. Her gaze shot to his, then past him, making sure no one was within earshot. "There's more to talk about than the fact that we did it or why."

"What do you mean, 'why' we did it?" he asked in a low, rough voice, stepping closer. "I did it because I wanted to, and so did you."

She gave him a flat stare, trying to dismiss the sensation prickling her skin. "Fine," she said tightly. "Let's talk. There's more between us than chemistry or attraction or—"

"Lust," he suggested.

Her stomach dipped. "Whatever you want to call it, there's something else."

"Like what?" Wariness tightened his features.

She was going for it. She wanted answers and he had

them. "Like the fact that you screwed up my life and I want to know why."

"Hell! Why do you have to bring the past into it?"

"Because until I get answers, the past is where we are."

He looked as though he wanted to argue, but he didn't. A muscle flexed in his jaw. Shoving a hand through his hair, he turned away.

"At the time of my wedding, you had just found out your wife was cheating on you. You had to be angry, bitter. Completely down on marriage."

Hands braced on his hips, his body went rigid. He looked over his shoulder, blue eyes piercing. "So?"

"Is that why you convinced Kyle to K.O. the wedding? Because what happened to you soured you on the whole idea of marriage? It would be understandable."

"No." He faced her, pinching the bridge of his nose. "It had nothing to do with me or my marriage."

"Then what?"

Looking grim, he met her gaze. There was no mistaking the reluctance on his strong features.

"Why did you stop my wedding, Houston? Why did you convince Kyle to leave me at the altar?"

"You deserve to know—"

"Then tell me."

"I'm not sure I'm the person who should do that."

"Well, who else? It's been five years and I've certainly gotten nothing from Kyle." She waited, fighting the urge to demand answers, to shake him until he gave them to her.

Couldn't he see how important this was? How desperately she needed to know?

Looking resigned, he gestured to the small room where they stood. "Sure you want to do this here?"

Her heart sped up. "You're really going to tell me?"

"If that's what you want."

"Now?"

"No time like the present," he muttered, looking as though he would rather face a disciplinary hearing.

After five years, she was finally going to learn the reason Nate had destroyed her wedding. Along with a sense of satisfaction, she was surprised to realize there was also a small bite of apprehension. "Let's go to the stairwell."

She picked up the folder holding Bane's e-mails and walked out with Nate into the hall. Unease vibrated from him with each step toward the putty-colored door leading to the stairs. They both reached for the pressure bar at the same time. His hand inadvertently covered hers.

Robin studied his face for a long moment before letting go and stepping inside.

Nate closed the door quietly behind them. Her hand had felt so small beneath his, so delicate. He did not want to be the person who told her this, but she deserved to know. He couldn't keep her in the dark the way Kyle and her sister had.

Not only because it was wrong, but also because he worked with her. He respected her. He liked her.

And there was that kiss, which took things to a whole different place. She had been clear about not wanting to discuss it, but at least she hadn't tried to pretend she didn't know what he was talking about when he brought it up.

Her dark honey taste, the deep velvet heat of her mouth, those too-brief seconds of surrender had knocked him for a loop. He had wanted more, still did. And despite her inscrutable cop face, she had wanted it, too. He could still feel her hand tighten on his thigh, the way she'd melted against him.

Nate wouldn't mind seeing where that kiss led, but he was pretty sure Robin wouldn't take it anywhere. Especially after this conversation.

"Houston," she said impatiently.

"Give me a second," he snapped. "It's not something I can just spit out."

She didn't say anything else, but he could tell it was killing her to stay quiet. How to start? There really was no tactful way to say it, no way to soften it so it wouldn't sound as devastating as it was.

She stood in the corner, her wary gaze locked on his. He eased back against the stair railing where two flights met.

"Right before your wedding was supposed to start, none of the groomsmen or the reverend could find Emrick. We split up to search the church, and I found him in the pastor's office." Nate saw her eyes darken with apprehension and his chest went tight. *Dammit, just tell her.* "I walked in on him having sex with another woman."

She stilled, the color draining from her face. The raw hurt and disbelief in her face had him stepping forward, reaching out to steady her with a hand under her elbow.

Nate hated this. *Hell!* "I'm sorry."

Tears glittered in her eyes. After a long minute, she exhaled shakily. "Wow, I'd say that's a good reason to interfere in someone's wedding."

"I didn't want to."

"Where were they?"

He frowned. "I told you."

"No, I mean on the floor, on the desk, standing up."

"Robin—"

She straightened, her voice crisp. "Tell me everything you saw. Everything."

"Do you think that's a good idea?" Nate asked softly. He sure as hell didn't. Wasn't this information hurtful enough already?

He could actually see her mask the stormy emotion in her eyes, blank her face as she went into cop mode. She was in total control. "Tell me."

Nate didn't want to, but after five years of wondering, it was way past time for her to know everything. At the steely look in her blue eyes, he said, "They were on the desk."

"Did you see who the woman was?"

"No, I could only see Emrick's bare butt and a woman's leg around his hip."

She thrust the folder at him and reached for the door.

Startled, Nate snagged her arm. "Where are you going?"

"To find Kyle. You're right. You aren't the one who should be telling me. He can look me in the face and give it up."

"Want me to go with you?" Nate didn't want to, and he knew she didn't want him to, but he felt compelled to offer, to do *something*. It seemed wrong to let her go alone. Especially considering how much worse the news could get if Kyle told her about her sister as he should.

"No, thanks," she said with quiet resolve, her features pinched with pain, betrayal as she walked out.

Nate grabbed the door before it squeezed shut and

stepped into the hall, watching her stalk toward the traffic division.

That first flare of anguish in her eyes had ripped right through him. Even though he had done the right thing, it still tore him up. For a few seconds, she had seemed so fragile.

This was between her and Kyle, but it grated on Nate to know she would face the bastard alone.

He had just reopened the wound of her past. Confronting her ex-fiancé would make a new, deeper wound. As unflappable as Robin was, the news about her sister would shake her.

Should he go after her? Wait for her?

He could write up his notes from the Jarvis interview, call and update McClain about what had been learned in the case today. Maybe by then Robin would be back.

Robin was so angry she could have chewed through metal. That lying, cheating SOB. The overwhelming urge to hit Kyle forced her to stop outside the traffic division and wrestle her composure back into place. Her chest felt as though it might explode, and she didn't want to see Kyle until she was in complete control.

After a moment she walked in, only to find his desk empty. A quick glance at her watch showed his shift had ended over an hour earlier. Now she really wanted to hit something.

Dan Rhodes, a wiry, ruddy-faced cop, walked up beside her. "You lookin' for somebody, Daly?"

"Emrick, but I just noticed the time. His shift is over, so he's probably already left."

"Saw him heading out about two minutes ago, if that helps."

"Thanks." She took the nearest exit, a back door at

the end of the hall that led out to parking spaces at the side of the building.

Scanning the small lot, she saw him in the far corner under the shade of a big oak tree. He sat on his motorcycle, nuzzling a cute redhead who stood between his legs. Robin bit back a sound of disgust. He had barely separated from his wife, the pig.

She wondered how long he had been sleeping with the woman Nate had caught him with at her wedding. A quick playback of their entire dating life flashed through her mind. She didn't remember any suspicious behavior, not once.

Neither Kyle nor the woman noticed Robin until she stopped within a few feet of them.

The redhead glanced over and stepped away from Kyle. "Hi, Detective."

Emrick smiled, the warmth in his eyes suggesting he was genuinely pleased to see her. It made her sick. He got to his feet. "Hey, Robin."

She recognized the redhead as the dispatcher who had worked at the Presley P.D. less than three months. "Maura, would you mind giving me a minute with Officer Emrick?"

Robin thought she sounded remarkably calm for wanting to smash his face in.

"Sure." With a wave at Kyle, the other woman walked away.

Robin noticed his gaze moving slowly up her legs, over her breasts to her face. His smile faded when his eyes met hers.

Looking wary, he took a step back. "What's going on?"

"We're going to have the conversation you owed me five years ago."

He tensed, glancing around. "Not here."

She gave a harsh laugh. "Trust me when I say that this is the safest place for you."

His broad shoulders grew rigid. She knew he still ran marathons. You'd think that kind of discipline might spill over into other areas of his life. He was a good-looking man, and that was about all there was to him. Robin had learned years ago that there was no character, no integrity under all the pretty wrapping. She'd been an idiot not to have realized it before she had agreed to marry him. Or—and here was a thought—when he jilted her.

"You've been thinking about our wedding?" he asked tightly. "Why are you bringing this up now?"

"The question is why didn't you tell me the truth five years ago? That you had sex with someone on our wedding day."

He blanched, an unfamiliar expression skittering across his face. If it had been anyone else, she might have thought it was shame, but not Kyle.

She balled her hands into fists, fought to keep them at her sides. "Nice to know you aren't denying it. How long had that affair been going on?"

"That day was the first time." He shifted uncomfortably, his face now chalky white. "So she finally told you."

She? She who?

"I told Wendy she was the one who owed you an explanation."

"Wendy? Why?"

The stricken hollow look on his face scrambled Robin's thoughts just before realization slammed into her like a truck. She froze; her stomach roiled. Surely he wasn't saying… "Wendy?"

The woman Kyle had been having sex with on their wedding day was her sister.

Wendy.

Before Robin was even aware of moving, her fist shot out and clipped him on the jaw. Hard.

His head snapped back and his eyes narrowed as he rubbed at the spot. "I guess I deserved that."

His words only made her want to hit him again. It was all she could do to get a full breath around the searing, razor-edged pain in her chest. "When did y'all hook up?"

"After the rehearsal dinner."

"First time with her?"

He nodded.

"Who else? Who else were you sleeping with while we were together?"

"No one. Just her."

Did it really matter how many women he had been with? Robin knew now about the one who mattered the most. The one who hurt the most.

Her sister had been his lover while he was with her. A greasy knot formed in Robin's stomach. "Both of you owed me an explanation," she ground out.

"I kept telling her that, but she didn't want to."

"Which is no excuse for *you* not to tell me."

Kyle had thrown away what Robin had thought was a good relationship twenty-four hours before they were to exchange vows. All this time she had tortured herself over what had gone wrong, wondered for a while if it was her. She replayed their time together in her mind so many times, she had worked a groove into her brain.

It hit her then, what he'd said. "What do you mean, you *kept* telling her to talk to me? Past tense. How long did you keep telling her?"

"A year."

"A. Year." Fury rolled through her like molten lava. Robin shook with the effort to not deck him again. "Does that mean you were sleeping with my sister for a year after you called off the wedding? Never mind. I know it does."

He stepped toward her and she glared him back. "I'm sorry."

"For what?" she scoffed. "Getting caught in the act?"

"No, for—how do you know we were caught?" Emrick's eyes went hard. "Houston, that sonofabitch. He's the one who told you."

Robin leveled her gaze on him until he glanced away. "He showed more respect for me on that one day than you ever did."

She was shocked to realize she really believed that. How easy it would have been for Nate to ignore what he had seen, keep silent and true to the good ol' boys code, but he hadn't.

"Thank goodness he walked in on the two of you. And thank goodness he had the guts to stop you from marrying me."

"I'm sorry. I really am. Ever since then, I've regretted it. I've wanted to tell you."

"If you had, you would've done it."

Regret crossed his handsome features, but Robin wasn't buying it. And frankly, she didn't care if he *was* genuinely sorry.

"I should've apologized years ago," he said. "I was an idiot."

"You got that right."

Her sister. Those two words kept lashing at her. Robin didn't want to believe Wendy had done such a thing, but she did believe it. She was angry at Kyle for what he'd done, angry at herself for not figuring it out, especially during the year following their aborted wedding. But the real devastation, the deepest betrayal, came from her sister.

Disgust filled her as she stared at Kyle. "I am so glad I didn't marry you. I feel sorry for the woman who did."

She turned to leave, trembling from anger, but holding it together.

"Are you going to speak to Wendy?"

She owed him no explanations. She kept walking.

"Robin?"

Tears burned her throat, but she swallowed them. She had done her last crying over Emrick long ago, but finding out about her sister made her feel as though her chest had cracked open.

How could Wendy have done something like this? Robin wondered briefly if their mother knew. No. If she had, she would have forced Wendy to confess.

Robin felt numb inside. She had to sit in her car a few minutes before she had herself completely under control. Loss and pain speared through her, but what drove the nail even deeper was that the affair had continued for a year. A year!

She was going to find out why Wendy had slept with Kyle, why she had continued to have an affair with him. As much as Kyle's betrayal hurt, it was nowhere near as heartbreaking as the fact that her own flesh and blood would do such a thing to her.

And Houston had known the woman with Kyle that day was Robin's sister. Why hadn't *he* told her?

She had every intention of asking him, but right now she couldn't handle it. She had to get out of there, away from everyone.

Chapter 7

Sitting at Robin's desk, Nate wrote out his notes from the Jarvis interview. That took about ten minutes. There was no sign of Robin. He called Collier and updated the fire investigator on what had transpired that day with the case. When McClain asked about Robin, Nate told him she was busy tying up some loose ends. After the phone call, she still didn't appear.

Nate supposed he should leave, but he couldn't make himself. He didn't *want* to. He wanted to see Robin, make sure she was okay after talking to Emrick. She hadn't asked him to stay, though. She hadn't asked him for anything.

He rubbed at the taut muscles across his nape. Nothing good could have come from her meeting with Emrick. Where was she? Was she all right?

Minutes passed, became a half hour. Then fifty minutes. Nate called his office, handled what business he could over the phone. A couple of times he went to the door to check the hallway then back to her chair. Finally, he couldn't stand it any longer. He had to see her.

Just as he stood and started around her desk, Emrick charged into the squad room.

"What the hell do you think you're doing?" the cop demanded.

Nate arched a brow. "I take it you aren't asking why I'm using Robin's desk."

"You damn well know what I'm talking about." Kyle stalked toward him, wiping away a trickle of blood at the corner of his mouth.

Nate noticed a bruise forming on the man's jaw. Had Robin done that? He bit back a smile.

Emrick got right in his face. "You bastard!"

Nate stiffened. "Back up. Unless you want a matching bruise on the other side."

The man didn't move away, but he didn't step closer, either. He glared as he rubbed his injured jaw.

Nate looked past Emrick into the hallway. "Where is she?"

"I don't know."

"What did you do to her?"

"I didn't do anything to her. *She* hit *me!* Why did you have to go and tell her, Houston?"

"Because you didn't," Nate said coldly.

"It should've come from me, not you."

"You had five years to tell her. Does she know about Wendy?"

The other man nodded and Nate bit off a curse. Finding out about her sister had to be killing her. *Where was she?*

Kyle glared at him. "None of this is your business."

"Thanks to you, it is. It was obvious the minute I saw y'all together earlier that you hadn't told her why you backed out of the wedding. You want to blame someone? Look in the mirror."

"I tried to apologize, but she just threw it back in my face."

"Go figure."

"I need to find her, try to talk to her."

"You mean try to convince her to forgive you?"

"Yes. If I could just talk to her—"

"Why don't you stay away from her?"

Still gingerly working his jaw, Kyle's eyes suddenly narrowed. "That's not your call, Houston."

"Maybe I can just take a hint." He looked pointedly at Emrick's bruised face and split lip. "A woman decks *me,* I'm going to give her some space."

"You probably couldn't wait to butt in, just like you did at the wedding."

A red mist hazed Nate's vision as anger erupted inside him.

"She deserved the truth, and you were wrong for not telling her. Just as wrong as you were to cheat on her in the first place."

"You think I don't know that?" Kyle muttered. "It's pretty clear there's no chance for us to get back together."

So, Nate thought, he hadn't misinterpreted the way Kyle had looked at Robin earlier. The man did still want her. What Nate wanted was to make sure she was all right. Concern gnawed at him. "Keep your distance from her, Emrick."

"Don't tell me what to do. I know I made a huge mistake."

"You sure did. Don't make it worse." Nate stepped

around him and out into the hall, striding toward the front exit.

Once outside, he stepped into the street and walked to his SUV. Daly could take care of herself. He knew that. And he'd just seen evidence of it on Emrick's face. Still, Nate needed to know for sure that she was okay.

He called her cell and got her voice mail. At her house, he left a message on the answering machine.

After two more calls to her cell phone, Nate went to the only place he could think Robin might be—the fire investigator's office. Maybe she was there talking to Terra Spencer. He knew the women were close friends.

By the time he walked into the redbrick building that housed Presley's fire investigator's offices, he thought if his shoulders got any more tense, they'd break.

The women weren't there, but McClain was. When he saw Nate standing in the doorway of his broom-closet-size office, a grim look settled on his face.

Nate lifted a hand in greeting. "Has Robin been here?"

"Yes, and she was pretty torn up." Collier sat back in his chair, his voice even.

Nate knew his friend was waiting for information before making a judgment, and since Robin was McClain's partner and his friend, Nate didn't have a problem giving it. He shoved a hand through his hair. "Do you think she'll be okay?"

"What happened?"

Nate shook his head. "That should come from her. I just need to know she's all right."

"Did something happen between y'all?" His buddy's mouth tightened. "Are you the reason she's upset?"

"No." At least, he didn't think so.

"But whatever is going on is personal, isn't it? Not about the Mailman or the task force."

Nate nodded. "I left her a couple of messages. She'll call me when she feels like it, I guess."

"Probably. She was holding it together when she left here."

Nate should've been reassured, but he wasn't. He wanted to see her for himself. Still, if she wanted anything from him, she would let him know.

He turned his attention to the green pressboard files spread across McClain's desk, the metal sample cans on the bookcase opposite the doorway. "Are you working the Mailman cases right now?"

Collier nodded. "Getting ready to add the information you gave me over the phone earlier."

"Mind if I go through all the files? Robin and I decided we should review everything, see if we missed something."

"Sure, help yourself." Collier pushed two thick files toward Nate.

An hour passed, then two, then three.

Nate pored over the files, looking for something, anything that might have been missed. As he laid out everything bit by bit, he didn't find any new information, but he became convinced that he hadn't mistakenly put away the wrong serial arsonist in Chicago. The accelerant and method of ignition were the same, but nothing else.

It was good to know Nate hadn't proved the wrong man guilty of killing his father and twenty-one other people. He might not have made a mistake with that case, but he was starting to wonder if he had made one with Robin.

It was after 9:00 p.m. when McClain said he was

ready to go home. Nate returned Collier's files and walked out with the fire investigator, who locked up. Robin still hadn't returned Nate's calls. The uncertainty of not knowing how she was handling everything flayed his nerves.

He couldn't quell an increasing sense of urgency to check on her. He had things to do, but until he saw Robin, he knew he'd get nowhere. She might not want company, especially his, but he had to know if she was all right.

He asked McClain for her home address, a place in the country outside Presley city limits. From his SUV, he called her cell phone again and got no answer.

He couldn't forget the bleak, stunned look on her face, the way the light had gone out of her gorgeous blue eyes when he had told her what Kyle had done. She'd been furious, yes, but also devastated.

Nate knew the feeling. He remembered the shock, the tearing pain he'd felt when he found out about his ex's affair, how lost he had been. Wondering, needing to know how Robin was coping, he started for her house.

Well, she had wanted answers. Now she had to deal with them.

It was almost 10:00 p.m. when Robin turned her paint mare back toward her house. She felt empty, flattened. She'd talked to Terra and Meredith. Then she had talked to Wendy. Or tried to. Just hearing her sister's voice made Robin's chest split open. Inflamed the anger and hurt all over again. She had hung up after Wendy had admitted to the affair.

Then she had slipped a bridle on Scout and taken off, sans saddle. Fifteen acres weren't a lot, but they were hers. They provided space and privacy, both of which she needed right now.

The pain and rage fused in a hot tangle in her chest, almost suffocating at times.

Loping back across the moonlit pasture, the rhythmic swish of grass brushing against the horse's legs took the edge off her emotions, though it didn't stop the darkness churning inside her. Her control was fraying. So far, she had managed to keep a tight leash on the turmoil, the fury, calling Wendy when she hadn't wanted to, asking questions when she really wanted to scream.

There had been a few tears when she had met Terra and Meredith for dinner, but she was handling everything. The way she always did.

So what if she felt raw and shaky? The emotions weren't owning her. As she reached the long metal gate she'd left open when she had come out to get Scout, she slid off the mare's back. The smells of horseflesh and grass and a faint whiff of earth surrounded her. Lightning bugs flashed in the silvery light like sprinkles of gold dust.

She was flooded with a sense of smallness, of vulnerability. Suddenly, the lock she had kept on her emotions busted. Reins in one hand, she dropped her forehead against the horse's hot damp neck.

She didn't know how long tears flowed down her face before she finally realized she was crying. Scout swung her head around and nudged Robin's arm as if asking if she were okay.

The scene Nate had described between her ex-fiancé and her sister in the pastor's office strobed through her mind. Every cell in her body ached. Robin felt disgust and anger at Kyle's infidelity, but she didn't think anything would ever top the vicious pain of knowing her sister had betrayed her.

It had happened five years ago. She didn't love Kyle anymore. She never had to see him again if she chose, but her sister was a different story.

"Robin?"

She froze, thinking she had heard someone's voice. A man.

"Robin?"

It was Nate! Scrubbing at her wet cheeks, she turned. The sight of him, so strong and big and…unscathed in the pale light brought back that initial rush of betrayal.

Her temper flared. "How did you know where I lived?"

"McClain told me."

"What are you doing here?"

"I came to see if you're okay."

"Sure, if by *okay* you mean knowing about my sister getting it on with my ex-fiancé."

"I don't like that you were hurt again, but I'm glad he finally told you the truth." Houston's eyes glittered like blue steel as he stepped closer. "That's a pretty good right hook you have."

Maybe she should feel sorry for clocking Kyle, but she didn't. "You saw him?"

Nate nodded. Looking wary, he gestured toward her. "I noticed you brought your gun."

Robin reached behind her and touched the weapon at the small of her back. He must have seen it when he came up behind her.

"You didn't come out here to use that, did you?"

He said it jokingly, but she saw genuine concern in his eyes. "On myself? Not hardly."

"Good." Relief was plain on his face.

"I might want to use it on you, though."

He stilled, his eyes narrowing. "You want to shoot the messenger?"

Earlier, when he had first broken the news about catching Kyle with another woman, she had been too rattled to follow up, but not now. "You knew the woman with Kyle was my sister."

"Not until a year later."

The image of Kyle and Wendy together had rage driving through Robin like a spike. "Why didn't you tell me earlier? At the police station?"

"I would have, but you shot out of the stairwell straight for Emrick."

"Why was it a year before you found out?"

"That was the first time I spoke with Kyle after the wedding. He called to see if I wanted some OSU football tickets and I asked if he had come clean with you yet." Nate watched her carefully. "That's when he told me who he'd been with the day of your wedding."

"Why didn't you let me know then?"

"He said he told you. I believed him."

"A cheater. You believed a cheater."

"Even if I hadn't," he said softly, "I couldn't just call you up and say oh, by the way, Emrick was doing your sister that day in the church."

"Why not?"

He arched a brow. "Would you have believed me?"

"Good point," she admitted grudgingly. She had thought Nate the biggest jerk on the planet back then. "Probably not."

But she also knew that if it weren't for him, she would never have found out. Tonight, Wendy had sworn she planned to confess everything at some point, but Robin didn't believe her.

Swallowing past the lump in her throat, she threaded the reins through her fingers. "What did you say that convinced him to call off the wedding?"

"That if he didn't tell you what he had done, I would."

She understood why Nate hadn't, understood he'd been lied to as well, but she felt a pang of hurt anyway.

How messed up was it that the man who had destroyed her wedding was the one who was with her right now? Checking on her, making sure she was all right.

Nate wasn't to blame for anything that had happened. In fact, his actions had stopped what would surely have been a disaster of a marriage. Her anger at him drained away and she had an insane urge to walk right into him and hold on tight. "I'm not mad at you. If it weren't for you, I still wouldn't know what happened at my own wedding."

She looped the reins over the mare's head, allowing the animal to graze for the time being. "I called Wendy earlier, but I couldn't talk long." Her legs felt weak, and she curled one hand into her horse's mane for support. "She apologized more than once, but I couldn't listen to her voice."

"Too soon."

The steady look in Nate's eyes reminded Robin he had experienced something similar.

"Yes. Every time she said she was sorry, it made me even madder."

Nate propped one hip against the wooden gatepost, hands in the pockets of his navy slacks. She noted absently that he still wore the same clothes he'd had on earlier. Hadn't he been home yet today?

As soon as she had gotten to her house, she had stripped out of her work clothes and pulled on an old pair of jeans and a tank top.

"She said she moved to Tulsa because she couldn't look at me without feeling guilty. She wanted to drive over tonight so we could talk face-to-face." Robin gave a half sob, half laugh, appreciating the understanding and patience in Nate's blue eyes.

"I'm not ready. The whole thing makes me sick to my stomach."

"Understandable," he said quietly, his voice a soothing rumble against the chirp of crickets and the slight rustle of wind through the grass.

"I suppose I should be glad she actually regrets what she—*they*—did, but it's too little, too late."

Robin's gaze locked on Nate's. What if she could never get past this with her sister? "Maybe I should've said I forgive her."

"You just found out three or four hours ago, Robin." He sounded impatient. Angry even, but she knew it was anger on her behalf, not aimed at her. He reached out as though to touch her, then pulled back and shoved his hand into his dark thick hair. "Give yourself some time."

"How much?"

"As much as it takes. Hell, woman, it took five years for them to tell you the truth."

"And it's only thanks to you that I found out at all. I do want to thank you."

He looked uncomfortable. "I wish I hadn't needed to say anything."

"So do I, but if you hadn't, I would've married the

jerk and he would probably still be sleeping with my sister," she choked out.

Tears welled in her eyes, spilled over despite her best effort to stop them. She swiped furiously at them. She didn't want to cry in front of him. She didn't want to cry at all.

Nate murmured something as he snagged her hand and tugged her into the hard length of his body. One strong arm slid around her waist. As much as Robin hated doing it, she buried her face against his chest, unable to stifle the sobs wrenching out of her.

To his credit, he didn't seem freaked out by her tears. His other hand curled around her nape, his voice soothing beneath the sound of her crying.

She should probably move away, but she didn't want to. For the first time since she had learned about her sister, she felt as though her world had stopped rocking. She had something solid to hold on to. Nate.

As much as it had hurt to learn the truth, Robin recognized full well that he had saved her from an even greater heartache and years of misery. Not only that, but he had tried to protect her from the hurt caused by her sister, too.

She pressed herself tighter against him, drawing in his tangy masculine soap, the scent of fabric softener. As much as she hadn't wanted to believe it all these years, he was a nice guy.

Warm, slightly rough fingers stroked her nape, melting away some of her tension. From above her, his voice came low and calming. "I didn't want to hurt you."

"I know." She flattened her palm against the steady beat of his heart. He had been protecting her for five years, still was. "I know that. You've been a good friend to me, even though I treated you like dirt."

"No, you didn't."

She pulled back to give him a look.

"Okay," he admitted with a half smile. "Once or twice."

"You could've turned your back," she said shakily. "Forgotten what you walked in on that day. No one would've known if you had kept it to yourself. The easy thing would have been to say nothing."

"After what I saw, I couldn't stay quiet."

A swell of fresh pain had her biting back a moan. "Sorry. I can't seem to stop crying. It was five years ago, for Pete's sake."

"You're entitled, sweetheart. What you found out was a betrayal of the worst sort, no matter when it happened."

Of course he understood, Robin thought. His wife had done the same thing to him.

"I know." She sniffed, wiping her eyes. "Doesn't mean I want to bawl all night."

"No one will know."

"You will." For some reason, the thought of that really bothered her.

"You just don't want anyone seeing you," he said with a grin. "It'll be our secret."

Another secret with him, like the elevator incident. Had it only been this morning when that had happened?

His gentle touch, his muscular arm around her was doing funny things to her stomach. She told herself to pull it together.

"Do you think this is weird?" Her voice was muffled against his shirt.

"That you're crying all over me?"

"All over the man who stopped my wedding?" *Who*

saved me. She could no longer think of him as the man who had ruined her life, could she?

"No, it's not weird. Well, maybe a little."

She gave a watery laugh.

With one hand still curled around her nape, he tilted her chin up with one knuckle, rubbed a thumb across her damp cheek. "Are you okay?"

"I will be." His touch set off a vibration deep inside her. And a staggering realization.

She felt stronger. Steady. Because of Nate. No man had ever done that for her. She was responsible for herself. Feeling this way about him confused her. Sent a burst of panic through her.

She stepped out of his hold, registering a sharp tug of longing at the loss of his soothing touch. "I just need some time to deal with all this."

As they looked at each other, a strange pulsing moment stretched between them.

The moonlight softened the blunt angles of his stubbled jaw, turned his eyes midnight blue. Dark. Dangerous. She wanted to touch him, stroke his face. More.

Why did she feel as if she were sliding out of control whenever she was with him? Just as she had in his truck earlier when he had kissed her. When *they* had kissed, she amended. She had been right there with him.

That had done as much to shake her up as what she had learned about Kyle and Wendy, albeit in a very different way.

If Nate kissed her again, she was afraid she wouldn't be able to resist. Or even want to.

As much as she might wish to, she couldn't ignore their kiss. "I also need some time to deal with what happened between us earlier."

He frowned, then realization spread across his face. "You mean the kiss."

She nodded.

He stared out at the night-silvered pasture. Finally, he looked at her. "You want me to apologize?"

"No," she said quickly.

Quickly enough that he gave her a slow grin. "Good, because I wasn't going to."

Heat flushed her face and she was glad he couldn't see how red it must be. "That's not what I meant at all. I just think it would be best if we kept our minds on the case for the time being. Stick to work."

"Business only, huh?"

"Yes." It sounded so blunt, so final. She didn't want that, but she kept it to herself.

Silence ticked between them. After a moment, he nodded. "You're right."

"I am?" The thoughtful look on his face had made her think he wanted to discuss it further or even protest. She must have misread that.

She squashed a flare of disappointment. Work only. This was what she wanted, what he said he wanted, so what was her problem?

She knew what it was.

She had severely misjudged him. What he had done for her showed the kind of man he was. The kind of man she hadn't expected. The kind Robin could easily fall for.

She shouldn't romanticize his actions. Because of his character, he likely would have done the same for anyone he thought was being treated badly. Still, it made him even more compelling. Harder to resist.

They had kissed and it had been great. Except for the part where she had felt completely unlike herself.

Reckless, wild. Helpless to say no the entire time his mouth had been on hers.

Robin didn't like that. At all.

Five years ago, he had turned her world upside down. She had vowed to keep a tight grip on the reins. And she had.

Until he walked back into her life and turned it upside down again.

Chapter 8

Three weeks later, Nate stood in the living room of Terra and Jack Spencer's house, along with about thirty other people attending a surprise party for Robin.

The birthday girl had told him she wanted things between them to be only about work for the time being. So far, the "time being" had been twenty-three days.

It wasn't that he was gauging the time that had passed since the day they had kissed. That had been day four of their working together, the day she had learned about her sister and her ex. Rather, he was aware of the time because he, like Robin and Collier, had been counting the days until the Mailman's next fire, and today was day twenty-seven. If the pattern held, there would be another fire tonight.

Nate had spent the last few weeks with Robin and Collier recanvassing neighborhoods, reexamining files and interviews, tedious grunt work. The times he and

Robin were together were all about the job. Tonight wasn't, and he wondered if he had made a mistake by coming, because the investigation wasn't holding his attention right now. But Robin was. She had been since she had walked in wearing a slim-fitting turquoise dress that skimmed her lush curves.

The bodice molded her full breasts then tapered in at her small waist, the gentle flare of her hips. The square neckline drew attention to a smooth expanse of rosy-gold skin and a hint of cleavage. Enough of a hint to make Nate sweat.

The whole picture—the sable cloud of hair sliding around her shoulders, her misty blue eyes, those spiked heels that made her bare, tanned legs endlessly long— had his chest going tight.

He again noted the scar on her right leg, pinkish beneath her tan. What had caused that? It sure didn't detract from how great her legs looked.

Gage Parrish's voice reached through the haze of lust. "It's amazing, the reason you finally caught that torch in Chicago was because his car tag was expired."

Determined to concentrate on the conversation with the former Oklahoma City fire investigator who now owned and ran a private arson investigation company, he nodded. "By then, we had identified our suspect, so when Chicago P.D. stopped him, the officer knew the guy was wanted."

"Gage has told me about the case." Meredith Boren Parrish walked up beside her husband, her gaze measuring. "Good work."

"Thanks." Nate hid his surprise at the compliment. At Robin's wedding, he had been the groomsman assigned to walk the blonde doctor down the aisle. As one of Robin's best friends, he figured Meredith thought he was dirt, too. He hadn't been sure what to expect when she had joined her husband and Nate.

"I've been following the Mailman cases in the paper." Gage slipped an arm around his wife's waist and they shared a look of pure joy, a look Nate had rarely seen between married couples. Certainly never between him and his ex-wife. "Sounds like you've got your work cut out for you."

Nate nodded then asked the other man about his business. As the conversation continued, Meredith occasionally participated.

Every couple of minutes, Nate found Robin. Once across the wide living room by the patio doors. Again as she moved toward the kitchen, stopping to chat with guests along the way. When she walked into the house, she had appeared genuinely surprised about the party. The open, unguarded smile she had given everyone had him wishing she would smile that way at him. And only him.

He dismissed the thought. They weren't going there.

Over the past week, the two of them had kept in touch about the Mailman cases, but as there had been nothing new, they and Collier had handled other cases or issues needing their attention. Nate had checked in each day with one of them, but this was the first time he had seen Robin in several days.

Though they had worked together just fine during those days, an underlying tension hummed between them. He knew it was because of their agreement to step back from that kiss. An agreement he had come to appreciate more with each passing day.

He would be lying if he said he didn't want to get naked with her, but he sensed there would be more than sex involved, and he *didn't* want that. One failed relationship was enough for him.

In addition to his keen awareness of her, there was a subtle but insistent strain that had to do with work. He felt it, knew Robin and Collier did, too.

As much as he hoped none of them got a call tonight about another fire-murder, he had a bad feeling in his gut.

Excusing himself from Gage and Meredith, Nate walked into the red-and-white kitchen for a beer. Collier and his brother, Walker, were there. Nate snagged a cold bottle of beer from a cooler on the floor beside the island and joined the McClain brothers. He knew Walker from a couple of pickup basketball games they had all played together. Their conversation centered around sports and Presley's upcoming Fourth of July parade.

Walker's wife, Jen, stood against a length of counter talking to Robin and firefighter Shelby Jessup. Nate wasn't sure of the connection between Robin and Shelby, but he remembered Collier telling him Robin and Jen had worked an undercover serial murder investigation together to try and determine if Walker had turned vigilante after the murder of his first wife.

Clay Jessup, whom Nate had met at the charity softball game, came in for a beer, stopping to chat for a minute before returning with his wife to the group in the living room.

After Walker introduced his wife, the couple wandered into the living room, leaving Collier, Nate and Robin in the kitchen. Just as he had done all evening, Nate searched her face for some sign in her striking features that showed how she was handling the information she had learned about her ex-fiancé and her sister.

He had met Robin's parents earlier when they

stopped briefly at the party on their way to a previous engagement. If Collier hadn't told him the Daly family had celebrated her birthday yesterday on the actual date, he would have thought it strange they hadn't stayed. Nate wondered if that family get-together had included Wendy.

Collier pulled a white chair from the nearby dining table and straddled it backwards. "Do we have anything new on Tiffany Jarvis? Anything to link her to the Mailman?"

"Not yet," Robin said. "The search warrant for her house didn't turn up envelopes, chlorine powder or petroleum jelly, nothing remotely connected to the accelerant used in these fire-murders, and we've had no reason to question her again."

Nate took another swallow of beer as he leaned back against the kitchen island. Only a few feet separated him and Robin, who stood across from him next to the refrigerator. The turquoise dress made her eyes even more blue.

Nate turned his attention back to their discussion. "The second interview Daly and I had with Sheila Bane's sister didn't get us any closer to proving Dennis Bane was having an affair. She didn't recognize Tiffany's name or face."

"Or Pattie Roper's," Robin put in.

That was the woman who had dated their first victim about six months prior to his death, Nate recalled. It was good that Robin still had the woman on her radar. "We've connected Pattie Roper to victim number one and Tiffany Jarvis to victim three, but that's it."

"If we could figure out the Mailman's motive, it would help," Robin said impatiently.

"I'm afraid we won't get a new lead unless there's

another fire-murder." McClain pinched the bridge of his nose. "I hate thinking more people will probably die before we catch this SOB."

Knowing it was very possible, Nate nodded grimly.

"Collier?" a feminine voice said quietly from the kitchen doorway.

Nate turned to see Kiley McClain motioning her husband over.

The big man chuckled. "My wife is paging me. See y'all in a bit."

Now alone with Robin, Nate studied her. He'd been doing a lot of that since she arrived this evening. Why not? It wasn't as though he was going to do something stupid and touch her. His libido was firmly leashed. He had kept his hands off her for three weeks. He could do it for three hours.

The air conditioner hummed beneath the din of voices from the Spencers' big front room. Scents of perfume and the outdoors and a heaping platter of chocolate chip cookies on the island mingled.

Nate and Robin were in plain view of everyone, and he was aware of the group of people in the other room, but he didn't really see anyone except her.

He'd been careful to keep his distance since she had walked into the Spencer house earlier in the evening, and it hadn't helped a damn bit. His whole body was tight.

His gaze locked on her mouth. The gloss of pale pink there made him want to kiss it off. He took a drink of his beer.

Her gaze searched his face. "I saw you talking to Meredith and Gage."

"Yes." Nate glanced into the living room and saw the couple with their hostess. "Terra said she was glad I accepted the invitation and Meredith didn't act as though she wanted to carve me into little pieces. I guess that's because of you."

She nodded. "I told them that you had been the one to tell me about Kyle and my sister."

"How are you doing with everything?"

"You mean Wendy?"

"Yeah."

When she looked away, he decided she must still not want to talk about anything except work. For some reason, that irritated him. So much so that he almost missed her next words.

"I think we need some ice. Terra told me there's an extra bag in the garage freezer."

As she started through the utility room, she looked over her shoulder at him and it finally registered she was inviting him along.

Pretty quick, Houston. "Need help?"

"Yes, thanks."

She wanted to talk privately. He ignored the voice telling him being alone with her might not be the best idea. Setting his half-empty beer bottle on the island, Nate followed her.

He closed the door quietly behind them and moved the few feet to the freezer in the corner. Even beneath the faint oily smell of car fuel and the outdoors, Nate caught her gut-twisting scent. Want slid under his skin.

He forced his gaze to the far wall where an assortment of yard tools hung from a Peg-Board. "How are things between you and your sister? Have the two of you talked yet?"

"No. She's still trying to get me to do that." Robin paused. "She was here last night for my actual birthday. We went to dinner with our parents."

"How did it go?"

"We were civil, but my parents sensed something was going on. When my mom asked what it was, I told her I wasn't ready to talk about it. I plan to take my time, like you suggested. If I don't, I'm afraid I'll do to Wendy what I did to Kyle."

Nate heard what she said, understood it, but he was distracted by the soft pink of her mouth.

She tucked a silky strand of dark hair behind her ear, looking up at him with a vulnerability and warmth that had him going still inside.

"The more I think about what you did, how you protected me, the more I'm...amazed. Touched."

"Robin—"

"Just say 'you're welcome.'"

"You're welcome." He was hit with a sudden need to put his hands on her, taste her again.

She edged closer and cupped his jaw. This past week, she had been restless, nagged by a vague sense of dissatisfaction, of wanting something. Tonight when she had seen Nate, she had known what. *Him.*

Unfortunately, she could tell he was going to continue doing what she had asked of him three weeks ago, and keep their relationship strictly professional. If things were going to change between them, she would have to be the one to take the first step.

The fabric of his red polo shirt stretched across his wide, muscular chest, had her fingers itching to touch him to see if it was as hard as it looked. As she drew in his scent, it seemed impossible to stop staring at his mouth.

She stepped toward him. "I told you I needed time to deal with what happened between us. Is that why you haven't asked me about it again?"

"Yes."

"Have you thought about it? The kiss, I mean."

"Yes. Have you?"

Encouraged by the frank male interest in his eyes, she nodded. "Do you think our agreement to stick to business only was smart?"

"Considering our track record with relationships, yes," he said carefully. "I don't ever want to go through the kind of hell caused by my divorce again. One failure like that is enough for me."

"Same here." Robin eased closer. "But I've been thinking about changing our agreement."

He didn't move.

Taking that as a good sign, she leaned into him, her breasts brushing his chest. A muscle twitched in his jaw. She looked up at him, suddenly breathless at the banked heat in his eyes.

It hit her then, that skittish feeling she had gotten the one time they had kissed. The sense of stepping off the edge into the unknown. But she was in control this time. She knew what she wanted. "What would you think about taking things to another level?"

"Define that," he demanded roughly.

"Getting naked."

His eyes, dark with desire, never left hers.

"Are you up for that?"

"Yes, but I don't do relationships. Note my divorce," he said wryly.

"That's on your ex-wife. You tried, and one person alone can't save a marriage. Besides, that isn't what I want."

"What then?"

"You. More." She smoothed a hand across his right

shoulder then lightly curled her hand around his nape. "No strings, just to see what happens."

He settled one hand lightly at her waist. "What about keeping things strictly business for the time being?"

"I think time's up," she said quietly, pulling his head down to hers.

He was prepared to let her control everything, but the first touch of her lips on his set off something inside him. Something wild and huge, primal, unfamiliar.

Wrapping one arm around her waist, he picked her up, backing her into the stretch of wall between the door leading into the house and the freezer. He held her tight to him, supporting both of them by bracing one hand on the wall.

After their first frantic taste of each other, he tried to slow down so he could savor the dark velvet of her mouth. The ragged moan spilling from her throat unleashed a raging torrent of heat inside him, a savage, overwhelming need to possess her.

Her arms tightened around his neck and her breasts pressed against him. He was fleetingly grateful for the wall at her back, because his legs felt like sand.

Dragging his mouth from hers, he buried his face in her fragrant hair, nipped her earlobe before moving down the length of her elegant neck. He touched his tongue to the hollow of her throat, where he could feel the wild beat of her pulse.

He wanted to take his time, enjoy the honeyed taste of her warm flesh, but the husky whisper of his name had hard, hot need ripping through him.

He fisted a hand in her hair, pulling her head back to take her mouth again, as he slid a hand up over her ribs and brushed his thumb across her taut nipple. He wished he could unzip her dress, see her naked flesh, but he was dimly aware that they could be interrupted at any moment.

The kiss changed, settled into a slow, giving exploration. She melted against him, every soft curve nestled against the rigid lines of his body. Damn, she felt good.

She drew away slightly, looking up at him with dazed blue eyes. Feeling dazed himself, he rested his forehead against hers.

She moved against him, her breathing as ragged as his. "That's what I was talking about."

Bending his head, he dropped a kiss on the bare skin where her shoulder met her neck. He nuzzled her jaw, her cheek. "I've been wanting to do this for a while."

"Me, too." Her lips met his in a deep, languid kiss.

One of her soft hands cupped his jaw, the other moved down his chest, then curled into the waistband of his jeans.

The muscles of his abdomen tightened in anticipation. He pressed her hips more firmly into his.

She went still.

Muscles tensed in frustration, he groaned. "What's wrong?"

Her mouth was wet and swollen from his. A wash of color stained her cheeks. "I think your phone is ringing."

Now he heard the low-pitched ring tone. It took a second for his body to cool down enough so that his brain could work. When it did, apprehension knotted his gut.

Another fire-murder? He read the same dread in Robin's eyes.

Keeping one hand on her shoulder, he fished the phone from his jeans pocket. His gut hollowed out as his boss confirmed his earlier apprehension. And even though Nate hadn't even seen the crime scene yet, he knew with sick certainty it was the work of the Mailman. When he disconnected, the same grim knowledge was in Robin's face.

"Where is it?"

"A summer camp for kids, outside Marshall City."

"Isn't that about seventy-five miles southwest of Presley?" At his nod, she asked, "Fatalities?"

"One. Caucasian male, early to midfifties."

"So, you have to go."

"*We* have to go, all three of us."

"Right." She shook her head, looking sheepish. "Right."

She flushed a pretty pink, and he was glad to see he wasn't the only one reeling from what had just happened.

"We should tell Collier," he said.

Her eyes were still soft with arousal. "I need to change clothes."

"That's a shame," he murmured. "Because you look great. Every inch of you looks great."

Standing this close to her, still touching her, made it difficult to slow his heart rate. Somehow he made himself let her go.

She turned to go back into the house, then swung around. "Oh, the ice."

"I'll get it." Nate reached into the freezer and grabbed a bag, then followed her slowly into the house, hoping like hell no one would notice his body's response to her.

Too bad he couldn't spend some time in that freezer. So much for keeping his hands—or anything else— off her.

He had an intense, extreme reaction to her on every level, not just the physical.

No woman had ever had such an effect on him. Ever. It was unwelcome. A little frustrating. A connection he hadn't ever experienced.

The fact that he had tried to protect her, then and now, from her lying, cheating bastard of an ex meant Nate had invested more of himself in her, with her, than he had with any woman since his ex. The realization had him sideways.

For the first time since his divorce, he had found a woman he didn't want to walk away from, but he wasn't sure he could stay, either.

During the entire drive to Spur Creek Camp, Robin's nerves were humming. If she and Nate had kissed much longer, she would have been ready to say yes to anything.

She had driven her own car because she probably wouldn't need to stay as long as he and maybe Collier. The men had ridden in Nate's SUV.

Since finding out about her sister and ex-fiancé, Robin had turned off as much emotion as possible, letting the pain and anger trickle in as she felt she could handle it. She had insulated herself, almost as though she'd been living in a bubble.

The instant her lips had touched Nate's, the bubble had burst. Sensation had flooded in. The feel of his firm lips against hers, the hard strength of his body, his strong arm wrapped so far around her that his fingers rested just beneath her breast.

Even before that scorching kiss in the garage, she had admitted she wanted him. She was able to do that because her perception of him had changed. At first because she had learned what he'd done for her at the wedding, and then as a result of working with him on the task force.

Now they had a new fire-murder. The Mailman had killed again, and the responsibility for that weighed on her. She knew Nate and Collier felt it as acutely as she did. And if she didn't get her head out of the clouds, this serial arsonist-murderer would continue burning and killing people.

As she drove under the iron arch entrance marked Spur Creek Camp, the acrid stench of smoke reached her. She topped a hill and started down the other side, her headlights cutting through the gray-brown haze drifting across the old tree-lined asphalt road.

Surrounded by woods, the camp was illuminated by lights mounted high on telephone poles. A large central building was flanked by six cabins on each side. A mobile home trailer sat under a sprawling oak. Between there and the main building was a long structure, which Robin assumed to be showers and restrooms.

The center building was burned away, smoldering in the blinding brightness of Nate's portable floodlights.

Three police cars, lights strobing, sat on the perimeter of the scene. She showed her badge to the closest officer and checked in, then parked her car behind his.

The firefighters had contained the blaze to this main building, and now the mess hall was propped up by charred and seared beams.

Stepping out into the sultry July night, Robin tugged on the steel-soled boots Collier had loaned her when they had investigated the first Mailman fire. The medical examiner's wagon sat near the mobile home, the open back door revealing a body bag holding the lone victim of this fire.

The wind, mostly blocked by the woods surrounding the campground, was heavy with smoke and swirling ash. Robin pulled her hair into a ponytail as she walked up to Nate and Collier, who stood at the edge of the burn area talking to a gaunt-looking man in a police uniform.

The man walked away as Robin approached. Nate gestured toward him. "That was Sergeant Hardin. He's going to have his officers fan out and search the area, see if they can find anyone hanging around. We've got one victim and one survivor."

"A survivor? Someone got out this time?"

"She was out of the building when the blaze started," Nate said.

"Hmm." Robin followed his gaze to a woman several feet away being checked for injuries by a firefighter. "Do we know the victim's name?"

"Hal Trahan," Nate answered.

Robin scribbled the name in her notebook. "Survivor?"

"Pattie Roper," Collier and Nate said quietly in unison.

Robin's head came up, excitement shooting through her veins. She saw the same emotion on the faces of both fire cops.

She studied the woman, noting how her jeans and T-shirt hung on her bony frame. Pattie Roper was skeleton thin. Robin recalled Billy Myers saying the woman he saw coming from his brother's apartment the night before the second fire-murder was "really skinny." Could it have been Pattie Roper?

Robin looked at Nate and Collier. "What did she have to say?"

"Don't know yet," Collier said.

Nate dragged a forearm across his forehead. A camera was slung around his neck and he held a microcassette recorder. A tackle box containing his hand tools sat at his feet. "We wanted to get the lights set up, then photograph the body and take measurements so the M.E. could move the victim."

Robin nodded, wishing she weren't so aware of the way his T-shirt snugged his hard biceps and hinted at the hard, muscular chest beneath the red fabric. The chest she'd been plastered to less than two hours earlier.

Reminding herself Nate was in charge, her gaze shifted to their lone witness. "How do you want to handle this?"

"You do the interview while Collier and I start working the fire scene."

"Okay." Slogging through red mud and trails of ashy water, she stepped carefully around the wood and glass littering the ground as she made her way over to Pattie Roper. Very interesting that her name had come up in connection with another fire.

The auburn-haired woman was pretty, but her features were drawn, her eyes reddened from tears and smoke. She coughed, wincing as though it hurt her throat. Smoke inhalation, Robin guessed.

Noting the woman's water bottle was empty, Robin took a full one offered by a firefighter and passed it to Pattie with a quiet introduction. "Why don't you tell me what happened."

"Hal and I were in the mess hall talking and I left to go to the restroom. There's one on the building's outside wall. When I came out, I smelled smoke." She paused, giving a sharp cough. "By the time I got to the back door, the fire was there. I ran around to a side window.

Flames were already there and at the front door, too. It spread so fast."

More than one point of origin, Robin concluded. "Were you and Mr. Trahan the only ones here?"

"Yes. We're between camp sessions."

Thank goodness there were no more people. The size of this place already gave Nate, Collier and Robin more than enough to cover. "So, why were you two here?"

"Someone close to me just died." Tears streamed down Pattie's face again. "Hal was…letting me cry on his shoulder."

The woman's hesitation made Robin think there was more to the story. "What was your relationship with Mr. Trahan?"

"We were friends. Tonight we decided to date," she sobbed, burying her face in her hands. "I'm sorry."

"Take your time," Robin offered. "It's no problem."

After a moment, the woman wiped her face with a tissue and nodded for Robin to continue. "Before the fire, did you notice anything unusual? Anyone else here?"

"No."

"Hear anything?"

"Like what?" she rasped.

"Some kind of transportation to or from here. Truck, car, a motorcycle."

"No."

So maybe the torch had come and gone on foot. Half turning to scan the wooded area around the camp, Robin asked, "Where would be the best vantage point for someone to watch the fire?"

"You think someone did this and watched?" The woman's voice trembled as she pointed across the camp beyond the glare of the floodlights. "There are two big red rocks past the last cabin. They mark the edge of the woods."

The spot was perfect, Robin noted. Close enough to watch the action and easy to disappear from if spotted. A natural-made sitting area. Yellow tape fluttered beyond the rocks, marking the space as within the crime scene. If there was anything to be found, Nate or Collier would find it.

During one of Pattie's coughing fits, Nate returned and drew Robin aside, saying in a low voice, "There are three points of origin and we found remains of a charred envelope and a gel-like substance on part of an exposed beam."

"Three points of origin matches what Pattie told me she saw. In the time she went to the restroom and returned, the fire started. The accelerant at the other fires ignited on its own. This one seems to have happened fast. If the accelerant had been there a long time, waiting for the petroleum jelly to seep through the envelope paper and reach the chlorine powder, wouldn't there have been some smoke or a burst of flame as a warning?"

"Yes, which means the torch combined the chlorine powder and petroleum jelly on his own, without waiting for it to seep through the envelope."

"Do you think it's the Mailman?"

"Yes." Nate's voice was hard, and so were his eyes. "This victim wasn't bound then burned in a bed, but that and the fast ignition are the only differences."

"I think it's the Mailman, too." And she was no happier than Nate about the bastard killing another person.

He thumbed a bead of sweat from his temple. His shirt and jeans were already streaked with soot. Robin had to stop herself from rubbing away a dark spot on the strong column of his bronzed neck.

She and Nate rejoined Pattie. "Do you have any idea who might do something like this? Kids? Disgruntled parents?"

"No."

"You and Trahan were here alone. Are either of you married?"

"We're both divorced."

"Anyone in either of your lives who might not like that?"

"Hal's ex-wife lives in Washington state and they never talk. My ex lives in Presley."

"Was your divorce amicable?"

"No," she said hoarsely, mopping at her tears. "It was bad. It's been bad ever since I filed. He's taking me to court to try for full custody. He's just doing it to upset me. He's hardly ever home. He works out of the state half of every month."

"What's his job?"

"He works on an offshore oil rig in the Gulf of Louisiana."

Before Robin could ask, Nate did. "What's his schedule?"

"Two weeks on, two weeks off."

Beside her, Robin felt Nate go as still as she did. Fourteen days on, fourteen days off. The twenty-seven-day pattern fell into that time frame. The Mailman could set up the accelerant on day twenty-six then head back to the rig the next day, getting him completely out of the state.

The look Nate gave Robin said he'd figured out the timing, too. Again, he anticipated her question to Pattie. "Does he spend his days off in Presley?"

"Yes. He wants to see the kids."

"When was the last time he saw them?"

"Last night."

Robin got a little buzz at the base of her spine.

"He's due back at the rig tomorrow for a new shift."

Roper's job fit the Mailman's schedule perfectly. This information had to mean something.

Trying to corral her excitement, Robin flipped to a previous page in her notebook and asked about the first victim. "We understand you knew Les Irwin."

"Yes." Pattie took a shuddering breath. "He was killed in a fire, too."

Nate tensed, his shoulder brushing Robin's. "Did you know a man named Brad Myers?"

The redhead shook her head.

"He owned a restaurant in Warren, Oklahoma," Nate said.

"Oh." A mix of embarrassment and recognition crossed the other woman's face. "I didn't know his name, but I—we—"

"Spent the night together?"

"Yes." Pattie coughed again, then took a long swallow of water.

So Pattie had known three of their victims. Trying not to get her hopes up, Robin continued where Nate left off. "Did you know Dennis or Sheila Bane?"

The other woman gasped. "Yes, Dennis and I were… friends. He's the person I was talking about earlier when I said I'd lost someone."

"Were you more than friends?"

After a slight hesitation, the woman nodded.

"Were the two of you having an affair?"

Pattie didn't answer. As the moment stretched out, Robin realized she was holding her breath.

Then the other woman's shoulders sagged. "Yes."

Yes! Finally, a bona fide lead. Barely able to contain a shout of joy, Robin exchanged a look with Nate. "Mrs. Roper, we can connect you to the victims of four fire-murders."

"What?" she asked in a thick voice. "What do you—" Horror flashed across her features. "Do you think I did this? I didn't! I couldn't!"

Maybe not. If Pattie was their arsonist-murderer, why had she stayed at the scene after the blaze started? Why call 911 then alert the camp's assistant director? The Mailman hadn't done any of that before.

"Maybe it's someone who knows you," Robin suggested.

For a second, Pattie looked blank. "I don't think I know anyone who would so something like this."

"You said your divorce was bitter. How bitter?"

"My ex and I don't get along at all, even in front of the kids."

"Does he know you have a pretty active dating life?"

The woman frowned. "I guess."

"So maybe he doesn't like you going out with other men," Robin said.

"Jealousy or revenge could be the motive." Nate's tone was low, for Robin's ears only.

Except for Sheila Bane, the victims had all been male, all sexually intimate with Pattie Roper. Maybe Sheila had died simply because she had been in the wrong place at the wrong time.

Robin leveled a look at Pattie. "We're going to need

to talk to your ex-husband. How do you get ahold of him while he's on the oil rig?"

Pattie sniffled. "He has a cell phone, but it doesn't work most of the time. The rig has a satellite phone. You can call that number and if he can't come to the phone, you can leave a message for him to call you."

"Could you give us the number?"

As the woman jotted it down, Nate excused himself to return to the burned building. Robin watched his smooth, purposeful strides, excitement rippling through her. The investigation was finally getting somewhere. She was elated about that, but the flutter in her stomach? That was all about Nate Houston.

Chapter 9

The next day, that flutter in her stomach had settled into a simmering anticipation. It probably wouldn't be going away anytime soon, especially since she and Nate were on their way to New Orleans without Collier.

He and Nate had stayed to work the fire scene through the night, while Robin had driven back to Presley and made airline reservations. The three of them had planned to interview Joel Roper today, but she had gotten a call from Collier before dawn, telling her he was at Presley's E.R. with his wife, who was being prepped for an emergency appendectomy.

When Nate and Robin had begun working together, she had been hot and bothered about being alone with him. She still was, but after their makeout session at her party, it was for a whole different reason. She didn't mind one bit that it would be only her and Nate for this trip.

Collier bowing out hadn't been the only development. He had found some evidence at Spur Creek campground that hadn't been at any of the other fire-murder scenes. On their way to the airport, Robin and Nate dropped it off for testing at the OSBI lab. The Oklahoma State Bureau of Investigation had a full lab whereas the Presley P.D. didn't.

It was late afternoon when they arrived in New Orleans and drove to a dock where a crew boat waited. It would take them the two miles from shore, out to the drilling rig where Joel Roper worked.

The steel-gray water changed to stormy blue as they left the shore behind. A fine mist covered Robin's hair by the time they approached the rig. The deck, a steel, open-frame design, sat atop four pylons. When they drew closer, Robin saw the structure was huge, a mass of cranes and machines. One of the crew members pointed out the individual modules on each level, which were for drilling and production equipment and living quarters.

The boat pulled up to the rig and a cylindrical basket with net sides and overhead protection dropped down. They stepped inside the "air tugger," which would transport them to the deck.

Robin swallowed hard at the thought of being suspended above the water. Just keep your eyes shut, she told herself.

Placing their feet in premarked places, Robin grabbed a rope attached to a center brace. There was water as far as she could see in every direction. A humid, salt-tinged wind skimmed across the ocean, whipping up frothy caps on the sun-gilded waves. Gulls swooped and called around the platform.

The tugger operator brought them up using a crane.

As they rose, the basket swayed in the wind. Nate remarked on a man dangling high above the water from a cable beneath the oil rig's platform. He appeared to be checking something. Robin kept her eyes closed.

Roper's boss, the drilling crew supervisor they'd spoken with earlier, met them on deck. The distance down to the water was greater than she had realized. He supplied the hard hat and safety goggles they were required to wear.

As they followed him through a maze of ladders and machines to an office module on the back side of the platform, he explained how the rig was fitted out almost like a cruise ship. All food, housing, laundry and travel were provided and paid for by the employer. In addition to the quarters and galley which served food twenty-four hours a day, there was a TV lounge, a weight room, even an area designated for smoking.

Smoking was allowed on an oil rig? She shared a frown with Nate.

The supervisor caught the look and explained, "We're conscious of the presence of combustible gases and materials. Employees can only smoke in a specified room, and they must use the safety matches we provide."

"Safety matches?"

"It means you can't ignite them using just any surface," Nate said. "You need the side of a matchbox or matchbook flap to start a flame."

Robin nodded as they were shown into a small office crowded with a desk, one chair, a computer and a long credenza filled with a fax machine, copier and an electrical log folded out to about a two-foot length. A man waited inside across from the door.

"You'll have some privacy in here," the supervisor said as he left.

Robin turned her attention to Joel Roper. Dressed in orange coveralls and safety boots, the leanly muscled middle-aged man had closely trimmed hair and weather-beaten, flat features.

Mud-brown eyes flared with concern when he saw Robin and Nate. "The boss said you were cops from Presley. Are my kids okay?"

"They're fine," Robin said.

"Then what can I do for you?" A look of irritation crossed his face.

"I'm Detective Daly and this is Agent Houston from the Oklahoma State Fire Marshal's office. We're investigating a series of arson-murders."

"What does that have to do with me?"

"Nothing, if your alibis check out."

"Why do I need an alibi?" His eyes narrowed. "Does my ex-wife have something to do with this? Is this her new way of trying to make my life hell?"

"No, our investigation led us here," Robin said. "But we have talked to her."

Nate added, "Now we're talking to you."

"Okay." A grudging look settled on his features.

Before Robin could start, Nate did. "Do you smoke?"

She knew he was asking because Collier had collected cigarette butts at the scene last night.

Roper's face went blank. "Used to smoke. Not any-more."

"What's your job here?" Robin asked.

"I'm a motorman. I do routine preventative main-tenance, minor repairs. Sometimes I operate a hydraulic pumping system."

"How do you get down here for your shifts?"

"Drive or fly."

"Did you know Les Irwin?" Robin asked.

"No. Who's that?"

"Our first victim," Nate answered. "What about a Brad Myers?"

Joel shook his head, giving the same answer about Dennis and Sheila Bane and Hal Trahan.

"Where do you usually spend your weeks off?" Nate asked.

"In Presley, so I can see my kids. I have an apartment there on the east side of town."

Robin watched his face carefully. "Would you be willing to let us search your place?"

"Why? You think I killed those people? I didn't even know them."

"Your ex-wife did, and she's the one person connected to all the victims."

"Then she probably did it," he spat out.

She gauged his reaction to her next words. "She's dated all those men."

"She's a slut. I don't care what she does."

"The murder dates all fall in a time period when you would've been taking your two weeks off shift, which you said you spend in Presley."

"If I was going to kill somebody, it would be Pattie," he said viciously, his face florid. "Not those people."

"Maybe you were jealous that your wife was seeing them," Nate said. "Or maybe you just wanted to get back at her for leaving and taking your kids. You're obviously bitter about it."

"It won't be long before I have my kids back," he muttered.

Robin arched a brow. "How's that? Are you planning to take your ex out of the picture?"

"I'm going to get full custody. My lawyer is petitioning the judge. All Pattie does is try to turn the kids against me. She's the one who shouldn't have them. She's not fit to be a mother."

Robin shared a look with Nate, who continued the questions. "Did you drive or fly back here for this shift?"

"Flew."

After he gave his flight number, she flipped open her notebook. "Where were you on April twelfth of this year?"

He frowned. "I have no idea."

"What about May ninth?"

"Don't know."

"June fifth?"

He shook his head.

"July second."

"On my way back down here."

"What time was your flight?"

"Ten o'clock last night."

Which would have allowed Roper to manually ignite the fire at Spur Creek and get to the airport in plenty of time for his flight.

"So you have no other alibis? Maybe you did something memorable with your kids on one of the other dates?"

He gave her a flat stare. "I don't remember the specific dates. I didn't know I needed an alibi."

Nate eyed the man. "All the fires we're investigating have been twenty-seven days apart. Your shift schedule matches the time between these fire-murders."

"Well, I didn't do anything," Roper snarled.

"You could help us eliminate you as a suspect by giving us a DNA sample," Robin suggested.

"The only thing I'm giving you is my lawyer's phone number. Now I have to get back to work. You're making me look bad in front of my boss, and I can't afford to lose this job."

He stalked around the desk and out.

Frustrated, Robin glanced at Nate. "What do you think?"

"I'm thinking about that smoker's room."

"Roper said he didn't smoke anymore."

"We should check it anyway and see if we find any cigarette butts."

"Good idea."

Fifteen minutes later, they reboarded the air tugger. Nate carried a small brown paper sack of the cigarette butts they'd found.

The wind had picked up since their arrival. As the crane operator began to lower the basket, it swung out then back. Squeezing her eyes shut, Robin tightened her grip on the rope attached to the center brace as they hung suspended over the dark water.

A gust of wind swept through, jerking the basket side to side. She had no time to recover from the whiplash-quick movement as the tugger continued to drop. The lurching descent started the world spinning and the bottom of her stomach dropped out.

She gripped the rope so tightly it burned her palm. She felt her legs give, but something steadied her. Nate. He had reached over to press a supporting hand to the small of her back. He couldn't move from his spot or he would upset their balance, but it helped.

She couldn't open her eyes, but her senses narrowed to him and only him. The possessive hand low on her back, the warmth of his body. When the basket sat down on the boat's deck, he stepped off.

His going first gave her a moment to get her bearings. If the trip had been longer or rougher, her vertigo probably would have been as bad as it had been the day of the elevator incident.

Nate offered her a hand and she stepped into the boat. She gave him a grateful smile. The wind ruffled his dark hair and she wanted to run her fingers through it.

When one corner of his mouth hitched up in a grin, she felt dizzy for a whole other reason. Their gazes locked.

By the time they reached the dock, she thought she had her balance back. But when she touched solid ground, her legs wobbled.

Nate stopped right beside her at the end of the ramp, his shoulder providing support. All she needed was a couple of breaths. She hated this. The clammy skin, the sudden spiral of the world around her. She hoped he didn't make a big deal out of this.

"We didn't get very far with Roper," Nate said.

Grateful he didn't comment, she smiled. "If we find his DNA on those cigarette butts Collier found, maybe we can match it to one of the butts we collected on the rig."

"He said he didn't smoke anymore." Robin realized Houston was giving her time to regain her equilibrium. "Maybe he started up again?"

"Maybe he saw his ex-wife with these men and his stress climbed each time he set a fire. Then last night he fell back into the habit."

"So we might actually get his DNA off those cigarette butts we took from the rig. We just don't have anything to compare it to."

"Yet," Nate said.

"Yet." The spinning sensation eased. "It doesn't look good that he won't give us a sample, but that could just mean he doesn't believe in helping the law. There are a lot of people like that."

As they started for the rental car, he asked quietly, "You okay?"

She knew he was referring to her vertigo. "Yes, thanks."

She *really* liked this man. Not just because his kisses turned her bones to wax, but she simply liked him. His level head, his dedication to the truth, even when it might make him look bad.

She was ready to do something about the electricity between them. She hoped he was, too.

Several hours later, Robin and Nate were back in Oklahoma, and on their way to his house.

Hitting the far northwest edge of the Presley city limits, she turned west off the main road. Beside her, Nate stirred. She glanced over to see him scrubbing a hand down his face.

They hadn't talked much on the flight from New Orleans. He had fallen asleep as soon as the plane had taken off. The man had to be exhausted.

"Do you think it means anything that Roper switched to an earlier flight?" Robin braked at a stop sign on what had turned into a two-lane road.

She and Nate had stopped at the ticket counter on their way out of the airport and luckily they had found an agent to ask.

"Him changing his flight to one that left only an hour and a half earlier than his original one does make it appear he was anxious to get out of town, but he might not have done it for a suspicious reason."

"Or," Robin said as she slowed to turn off the paved road onto a gravel one, "it might mean he was trying to get the heck out of Oklahoma altogether, as fast as he could, not just away from the fire scene. His ex-wife wasted no time calling 911."

Nate nodded, his attention trained somewhere in the distance.

"We may never know. Sure can't prove anything either way."

Again, he simply nodded. She frowned over at him, trying a different topic. "When you spoke to Collier earlier, how long did he say Kiley had to stay in the hospital?"

He didn't appear to have heard her, but just as she started to ask again, he said, "Through tomorrow."

Gravel crunched beneath the tires, dust swirling around the car. White PVC fenced the moonlit pasture on both sides of the road. Nate was too quiet. At first Robin assumed it was because he was tired, but she sensed something else now. Something was bothering him.

Maybe the case? Or maybe he was thinking about what had happened between them last night, before they had responded to the fire call? She had certainly thought about it.

She took in his strong, muscular thighs gloved by worn denim, the long-sleeved blue shirt with the cuffs rolled back to reveal forearms dusted with dark hair. Remembering how that hard chest felt against hers, the solid steel of his shoulders beneath her touch, her gaze followed the angle of his stubbled jaw, his corded neck.

His clean male scent mixed with the faint floral of her shampoo and her pulse jumped. She wanted to take a big bite of him.

Their makeout session at her party seemed ages ago. She realized then he was watching her thoughtfully. Was his mind going down the same path?

"What are you thinking about?" she asked. "You seem distracted."

"Those Roper kids. Their parents' divorce sounded like hell."

Boy, had she been far off the mark. She stopped the car in front of his gray stone house. "I guess you know exactly how they feel, huh?"

"I hope they don't have to go through what my sister and I did."

She killed the engine. Large windows glittered across the front of the traditional style house. With a wide porch, the structure nestled in the middle of mature, sprawling oak and maple trees. During the day, they would provide shade on every side of the house.

"Why was your parents' divorce so bitter?"

"It was just like their marriage. As far back as I can remember, they never got along."

"Why did they get married in the first place?"

"Because my mom got pregnant with Becca. My sister had overheard them say more than once that she was the only reason they got married, so when they split up, she felt that was because of her, too."

Robin felt a pang in her chest. "What did you think?"

"At first I thought it was because of both of us. It took me years to understand it really had nothing to do with us. It took Becca longer to accept that, but she has now. They used us as bargaining chips, put us right in the middle."

Robin's throat tightened, as she shifted in her seat. "And that's why you were so determined not to get a divorce."

He nodded.

"I know your dad's gone. How do you and Becca get along with your mom?"

"Fine now. Mom finally realized what they had done to us. She went for counseling, which helped everyone. Then she met my stepfather, Bob. He was a good man."

"Do you still resent your parents for drawing y'all into their fight like that?"

"No. Not most of the time anyway. When Becca and I saw how good Bob was to our mom, how happy she was, we realized how miserable both she and our dad had been. They felt trapped." He shrugged. "It was a long time ago. Things are fine now."

"Still, those family hurts go deep."

He looked at her. "Like you and Wendy."

"Yes." Robin was still in pain over her sister's betrayal, probably always would be, but it didn't have to ruin the rest of her life, did it?

Nate's gaze softened on her face. "It took a lot of years to put things back together with my parents, but I was really glad we did, especially when my dad died while fighting that fire. One minute he was here, the next he wasn't."

"I bet."

"My sister and brother-in-law have gone through some rough patches, but they're still together. Becca was able to stick it out when I wasn't."

"Nate, you *did* try to stick it out." Robin angled

toward him, her knee touching the center console. "Your wife had already left you for all practical purposes."

"I've been glad more than once that we never had kids."

"Would you like to someday?"

In the shadows, she couldn't read his expression. It took him a moment to answer. "Possibly. What about you?"

"I haven't thought about it since the disaster with Kyle, but maybe."

"Would you ever consider marriage again?" He sounded thoughtful.

Surprisingly, his question didn't fill her with cold dread, as it once would have. She didn't know what to make of that, but she knew she didn't want to talk about it. She waved a dismissive hand. "How did we get on that subject?"

"Tell me."

His husky words put a shimmer in her nerves. "I don't know. What about you?"

"I used to think absolutely not. Now I don't know, either."

Some invisible connection snapped tight between them. She gave a nervous laugh. "Neither one of us is sure about much, are we?"

"I'm sure about one thing," he said softly, his gaze dropping to her mouth. "I'm real sure."

He curled a hand around her nape and pulled her to him, his mouth covering hers.

Oh. She was sure about this, too. Robin relaxed against him.

He angled her head so he could go deeper with his tongue. Flattening one hand on his hard, hot chest, she held on to his waist, trying to get closer. This wasn't close enough. It wasn't enough of anything.

He pulled back, his voice gruff with need. "We have some unfinished business."

"From the party?"

"Yes."

Anticipation unfurled inside her. "You're not too tired?"

"No." His features were taut with desire.

The arousal glittering in his eyes made her flush. She felt a twinge of panic, as though what was happening with them was bigger than she was.

"Come in," he said roughly, threading his fingers through hers. "Stay. Whatever is between us isn't easing up. It's just getting stronger."

"I'm tired of fighting it," she admitted. Was that her voice, husky and breathless? Yes, and there was nothing other than flat-out lust going on here. Period. Her hormones were being stirred up more than they had in years. She had it under control. "Okay, I'll stay."

They got out of the car and she met him on the other side to walk with him to the front door. Time seemed to stretch as she waited for him to unlock the door. She was dimly aware of the chirp of crickets. The soft glow of the porch light slid across Nate's bluntly squared jaw, had her lifting her hand to touch his face. This man could be lethal to her heart.

She immediately dismissed the thought. Get real. What was happening between them had nothing to do with her heart.

Nate pulled her to him and turned the knob. She had made the first move last night. He had no problem making the next one.

His kiss was slow, until Robin went soft in his arms.

He picked her up and carried her inside, kicking the door shut and pressing her into the wall.

Working his hand under her T-shirt, he skimmed up the warm satin of her torso to cup her breast, thumb her tight nipple through the lace of her bra. He needed to see all of her.

Making a ragged sound, she moved against him, pulling off her top as he slid one hand around to unfasten her bra and push it off her shoulders.

Lush, creamy breasts, taut, pale nipples had him bracing himself against a savage rush of need. Keeping her against the wall, he stared in arrested silence as he closed his hands over her.

She tugged his shirt out of his jeans, managed to open one button, then two, three. Jerking at the fabric, she blew out an exasperated breath. "Nate, help me."

He didn't want to let go of her, even for a second, but he wanted to feel her naked body against his. He wasn't wasting time with the damn buttons. Reaching back, he pulled the shirt over his head, dropped it.

She came into him, pressing her bare breasts against him. He thought she said something, but if so, it was lost beneath the roar of his heartbeat.

He unsnapped her jeans, pushed his hands inside her panties to curve over her bottom. The feel of her firm, silky flesh beneath his rougher skin wound him up even tighter.

Robin slid her hands up his arms to his shoulders, as she lifted up to kiss him and rake her teeth down his throat. He wasn't going to last much longer.

He pushed her underwear down along with her jeans, kneeling to help her get them off. As she kicked the clothes away, he ran his hands up the backs of her thighs, inhaling the intoxicating scent of flowers and woman.

When he rose, Robin struggled with the button of his jeans. She made a sound low in her throat. "You are one hard man to get naked."

He chuckled, closing his mouth over her breast as she got his fly open. When she reached inside and curled a soft hand around him, Nate had to clamp down hard on the savage need clawing to break loose.

Driven by an urgency bordering on desperation, he cupped her between the legs, curled his fingers up inside her. She was hot and soft and wet.

"Here?" he groaned. "Now?"

Please let her say 'yes,' because he didn't think he could move from this spot. Or wait.

"Yes," she said breathlessly.

He pulled back to look at her. Moonlight streamed through the front windows, washing the foyer in hazy silver and turning her skin to delicate porcelain. Her eyes were hot blue and needy, her breasts damp from his mouth.

As she worked his jeans lower, he lifted her. She wrapped her legs around his waist and began to sink down.

"Wait." He gripped her hips, his head falling forward as he hissed out a curse. "Condom. Back pocket."

"I've got it." She reached around and pulled out his wallet.

The fever in his blood scrambled his brain. They were lucky he had even managed to think about protection.

He heard the tear of the packet and looked down. The slow stroke of her hands as she sheathed him had Nate gritting his back teeth. "Hurry, damn it."

"I am— *Oh!*"

He slid inside hard, deep.

"Nate."

The broken sound of his name went through him like a flash fire. He buried his head in her fragrant hair, trying to hold back, but he couldn't. The feel of her sleek, tight warmth obliterated everything else. He moved. He had to.

And when he saw she was right there with him, he tilted her hips and brought her even closer, finding the small nub at her center. They went over the edge together.

For long moments, they stayed against the wall, their bodies slick with sweat. Only after their pulses slowed did Nate's legs work.

Finally, he carried her into his bedroom. They fell onto his big bed, on top of his navy comforter. Neither spoke. There was only the sound of their breathing and the promise of the night beyond. Moonlight streamed through his windows, rippling on the floor and wall like water.

He stared lazily at the tall chest of drawers in the corner, the TV and its cabinet at the foot of his bed.

Robin lay on her left side, right leg thrown over his lower hairy one. The pale light polished her velvet skin to ivory. Her dark hair rippled across her shoulder, tickled his chest.

He ran his fingers through the satin mass, stroked her shoulder with his thumb. "You doing okay?"

"Mmm-hmm."

The feel of her bare skin, hot and sleek against his, pumped through him like a drug. He shifted so he was on his side facing her. She was so gorgeous.

He stroked his knuckles up and down her arm. He couldn't stop touching her petal-soft skin, didn't want to.

His gaze trailed over her lush breasts, down her

slender thighs to her delicate feet. Reaching down, he pulled her leg higher on his, so that she rode his thigh and lightly touched the scar between her ankle and calf. "What happened here?"

"Got caught in an explosion."

When she didn't say anything more, he nudged her with his hips. "And?"

She looked up at him, her eyes drowsy and misty blue. "You met Shelby Jessup, right?"

He nodded, his breath hitching as her hand slid lower on his belly. "She witnessed a murder. When someone tried to kill her, she was put in protective custody and I was the officer assigned. One day, I took her to a meeting at an office building that wasn't quite finished. An explosion went off and we were caught in a fire. A piece of wood speared me. Had to have stitches."

"Ouch." Nate curved his hand over her calf, lightly grazing his thumb across the old wound. He could happily stay like this for at least the next twenty-four hours.

Rolling her to her back, he kissed her. When he started to do it again, she held him still.

He lifted his head, saw a flash of uncertainty in her eyes. His chest tightened. "You weren't planning to leave, were you?"

"I...don't know."

He kissed his way down her stomach to the jut of one hip, his shoulders pushing her legs apart as he settled himself between her thighs.

When his breath washed against her, she shuddered. "No, I'm not going anywhere."

"Good answer," he murmured against her inner thigh, smiling when she lifted to him.

He hadn't realized until that moment how badly he

wanted her to stay. They had agreed this was strictly physical, but as he held her, Nate admitted there was something else. He felt…marked.

He wasn't even sure what that meant. Or how he felt about it. Of course, there was no way in hell he would say any of this to Robin. She'd said to take things as they came, so he would.

Chapter 10

Last night, Nate had decided to take things as they came. So far, things were coming along just fine. The sex had been great, then and this morning.

His relationships since Stephanie had consisted of two dates with the same woman, three max, but this was different. He didn't have that raw edginess churning his gut, the urge to put some space between him and Robin. When they had stopped at the hospital for a short visit with Kiley and Collier, and to collect Nate's truck, he had wanted to pull her into the nearest supply closet and have her again.

His gaze traced over the lightweight, red-hot sweater stretched across her full breasts and the slim-fitting slacks in the same red. Sex wasn't the only thing they did well together. There was also work, which was why they were walking into Pattie Roper's office building this morning.

The towering glass and steel structure was even taller than the one where they had gone to interview Dennis Bane's coworkers. Nate watched Robin carefully as she read the directory attached to the wall between two elevators. Pattie was the accountant for a plastic surgeon whose office was located on the thirtieth floor.

Robin impatiently stabbed the button. Nate couldn't tell if she was nervous about getting on the elevator. "I can have Pattie come down here to talk to us."

Robin turned with a frown. "Why?"

"Because your vertigo might kick in."

"I had a problem with the elevator at Bane's office building because it was glass. This one isn't. I'll be fine."

She wouldn't admit it even if she weren't, Nate knew. In fact, she seemed almost annoyed that he had offered to ask Pattie to come to the lobby.

"Her office is thirty floors up. It wouldn't be a big deal for her to come down."

Robin's blue eyes flashed. "It's okay, Nate. I have vertigo, not a fear of heights."

"Vertigo that's sometimes aggravated by elevators," he pointed out.

"Not every time. You don't have to take care of me."

"All right." He didn't understand why she was so damn prickly, when he was just trying to help. "We'll go up."

A few minutes later, they stood in a surgery consultation room, alone with Pattie. Dressed in a sharp yellow sheath and cropped jacket, the auburn-haired woman had circles under her eyes. Her hair was pulled back, which highlighted the sharp jut of her jaw, the ashen cast of her complexion. Nate was reminded of how extremely thin she was.

Robin started them off. "We need to ask you where you were on the fire-murder dates."

"All right." Pattie pulled her cell phone from her jacket pocket. "I use the calendar on here. What's the first date?"

"April twelfth."

"I was at an accounting conference in Denver."

"May ninth?"

"My daughter's ballet recital."

When Robin gave the next date, Pattie scrolled down. "On June fifth I took the kids to my mom's for the weekend. She lives in Stillwater. And you know where I was for this last fire, at Spur Creek campground." She looked up from her phone. "Did y'all talk to Joel?"

Robin nodded. "He can't account for his whereabouts on any of the dates in question."

Alarm flared in the other woman's eyes. "Do you think he's the one who murdered those people?"

Rather than answer, Nate countered, "Would you happen to have noted if he was with the kids on any of those dates, or if there might have been something special that he attended?"

"Special? Like a school function?"

"Yes. Or sports—whatever."

Pattie looked at her cell phone again, then passed it to Nate, showing him how to scan through her calendar.

Robin leaned in to look with him, the sweet fragrance of her hair teasing him. He wanted to bury his hands in the dark, silky mass. And the urge to touch her that he'd felt since they had gotten up that morning hadn't gone away, just because they were handling business.

Pattie's calendar was well detailed.

"I notice you have certain weekends marked for Joel," Robin said.

"Yes, those are the ones ordered by the court, and he doesn't miss them."

Nate returned her phone. "Does he always take the kids to his apartment in Presley?"

"Yes."

"He never stays at your house with them?"

Her mouth tightening, Pattie shook her head. "I don't even let him come in when he picks up the kids."

Nate's mom had been the same after his dad moved out. Beside him, Robin shifted, the petal-smooth skin of her arm brushing his. "Is it possible Joel might have left something of his when he moved out?"

Good question, Nate thought admiringly, urging his mind to stay on the interview.

The other woman nodded. "There's a box of his stuff in the garage. It's with some other things I plan to give away."

"We'd like to take a look at it," Robin said.

Though Pattie looked surprised, she nodded. "Sure. Now?"

"Now would be great."

"Let me tell my boss what's going on. It shouldn't be a problem for me to leave for a bit."

Thirty-five minutes later, they stood in the Roper garage. After she pointed out a box between a cooler and an old light fixture, Nate pulled it down from the top of a metal shelving unit and opened it.

Robin leaned in close to see what was inside. There were a few old T-shirts, two mismatched socks, and a shaving kit.

Pulling on a pair of latex gloves, she opened the kit, then glanced at Nate. Excitement glittered in her eyes as she tilted the leather bag, showing him a razor, a toothbrush and travel-size shampoo.

Nate grinned.

"Will that help you?" Pattie asked.

"Yes," he said. "We'll need to take this."

"That's fine."

After thanking the woman for her help, Robin and Nate walked out. Once they were inside Nate's SUV, she smiled. "We may have just gotten lucky."

Nate thought he would like to get lucky with her, right now.

She must have read it on his face, because she rolled her eyes, muttering, "Dream on."

He chuckled, pulling away from the curb.

After leaving the shaving kit at the OSBI lab, they spent the rest of the day confirming Pattie's alibis and formally clearing her as a suspect. It was late afternoon before Nate brought Robin back to the P.D., where they had left her car that morning.

The sun was a glaring ball of yellow in a clear blue sky. As she started to open the vehicle door, her cell phone rang. She glanced at the readout and her mouth tightened. After a brief conversation, she hung up.

Nate frowned. "Problem?"

"Wendy."

"You guys haven't talked everything out yet?"

Stiffening, she shook her head. She didn't snap at him or even tell him to mind his own business, but he could read between the lines. She didn't want to talk about it, not with him, anyway. That was fine.

He took her hand, rubbing a thumb across her knuckles. "Do you want to go to dinner?"

"I don't think so."

He hadn't expected that. He studied her face, wishing

he could see her eyes behind her sunglasses. "Got plans?"

"Nothing fun. I've decided to talk to my sister tonight."

"That's good." He squeezed her hand. "Will I see you later?"

"Probably not until tomorrow."

He wanted her to spend the night with him, but they hadn't made plans. Or promises. "Everything else is okay?"

"Yes."

It would be difficult to deal with her sister, but Robin didn't appear to need or want support. "If you want to call me afterwards, then do, okay?"

She nodded. "Thanks."

He fingered a strand of silky hair laying across her shoulder, then cupped her nape and brought her close. He kissed her, his tongue dipping inside the hot velvet of her mouth. She slid her arms around his neck.

This woman was definitely different. Enough so that Nate was thinking about things with her that he hadn't considered since his divorce. He didn't stop kissing her until they were both breathing hard.

She blinked dazedly at him, dark color streaking her cheeks. "Wow."

"That has to last until the next time I see you," he said huskily.

"I would much rather stay here and do this."

After another kiss, she sighed and climbed out of his SUV. He watched her walk away. Along the way, a uniformed officer stopped to talk to her, making her laugh.

Suddenly feeling territorial, Nate realized he didn't want to see anyone except her. He didn't want her seeing anyone else, either. The thought that some other man might put his hands on her had him grinding his teeth hard enough to snap bone.

This was the first time since his wife that he'd felt anything soft for a woman, something other than temporary. He was willing to take things further and see if there was more than sex between them.

But what about Robin? Would she be interested?

He had considered bringing it up, until she told him she was planning to talk to her sister that night. The next time she and Nate were alone, he would ask, but not if Wendy's name came up. When he spilled his guts, he didn't want her sister anywhere in that conversation. Just him.

Three hours later, Robin found herself on Nate's front porch. She didn't question why she was there. Didn't want to analyze what had brought her to his doorstep. Had no clue why it seemed so important to come to *him*. All she knew was she had to see him, tell him about her conversation with Wendy.

Exhilarated, she rang his doorbell. After a few seconds, the door opened and he stood there bare-chested, wearing khaki shorts and running shoes. At the sight of all that taut, naked flesh, her mouth went dry. Helpless to stop, her gaze traced over the dark hair of his chest, the hard muscles of his stomach, down his powerful legs. She was hit with the urge to run her hands over every inch of him.

When she finally looked at his face, she found amusement in his eyes. Of course, he'd caught her practically drooling.

He grinned. "I thought I wasn't going to see you until tomorrow."

"I couldn't wait."

"As much as I wish that was because of me, I have a feeling it isn't."

"Part of it *could* be about you," she teased.

He stepped back to let her in, then closed the door behind her. The house was cool, after the sultry heat of the evening.

"Has something happened with the case?" His gaze did a slow hike over her white sleeveless blouse and navy shorts, down her bare legs to her sandals. Her belly dipped as his gaze returned to her face. "You look like you have news."

"I talked to Wendy."

"Yeah?" Looking curious, he started through his open airy living area toward the kitchen, motioning her to follow. "Want a beer?"

"No, thanks." The long, sleek lines of his back flexed when he reached into the refrigerator. She wanted to slide her mouth over the smooth, golden skin of his shoulders, but she hadn't come here for that.

Anxious to talk about her sister, she moved to the end of the kitchen island, laying her purse on the countertop.

Nate twisted the cap off a longneck, leaning his backside against the opposite counter. There was genuine interest in his blue eyes. "So, how did it go with Wendy?"

"I pretty much vented every thought I've had since learning the truth. There was a lot of yelling and crying, but we cleared the air."

Nate nodded. "Did she say why she slept with Kyle in the first place?"

Robin had expected the quick jab of pain in her chest at the reference to her cheating sibling and ex-fiancé.

That would fade with time. She was more focused on the here and now. And the big man in front of her. "She said she wanted him and he didn't say no."

"She *wanted* him?" His voice as incredulous as her own had been, he paused with the bottle halfway to his mouth. "That's her reason?"

"She said she was jealous of what I had, and it wasn't so much about hurting me as it was about taking what she wanted."

Eyes sharpening, a muscle in his jaw flexed. "That's splitting a damn fine hair."

"And it didn't make what she did hurt any less." She followed the line of dark hair down his torso, to where it disappeared beneath the low-riding waist of his shorts. His shoulders and biceps were huge, his muscles cut with definition.

"Robin?"

She hadn't come here for sex, but she was starting to wonder why not. She stepped over to him, laid a hand on his chest.

He put his beer on the counter and rested one hand on her waist. "What made you decide to talk to her?"

"When she called earlier, I knew it was time. I was ready to get it done."

He fingered a strand of her loose hair. "Good."

She leaned into him, both hands on his chest now. The feel of his powerful body against hers from chest to toe, the scent of musky soap and clean male had her stomach clenching. "I'm not sure what will happen with Wendy and me, but I feel as though I can start putting it behind me."

He linked both arms loosely around her waist.

"Our relationship was never great, but maybe we can build something stronger."

"And you want to do that?"

"If I never want to see Kyle again, I don't have to, but that isn't true of Wendy. I'm still hurt and angry. And I imagine there will be days when I have no desire to forgive her. But right now I feel positive. I didn't realize how much the issue was weighing on me."

One corner of his mouth hitched up as he lifted her slightly off the ground. "You feel lighter."

"Ha, ha."

He eased her down and tucked her hips tight against his. "Good for you. I'm glad the two of you talked."

She nuzzled his neck, her senses filling with his clean, masculine scent. "You smell good."

Hard and hot against her, his hands curved over her bottom. She rolled up on her tiptoes to brush a soft kiss across his lips.

He held her in place, his whiskey-smooth voice stroking every nerve ending. "What was that for?"

"For listening."

"If I get one of those every time I listen, then start talking."

Sliding her fingers into his thick, silky hair, she pulled him to her and kissed him again, tasting the faint bite of beer.

"Keep going," he rasped, before sliding his tongue into her mouth and taking over.

Something about him just fit her, in that deep secret place most people never reached. She flexed her hands in the crisp hair on his chest, his bare flesh hot beneath her touch. Sliding her palms up his iron-hard arms, she kneaded her way to his shoulders. There was no give in those muscles.

When her arms tightened around him, he dragged

his mouth to her ear, the tickle of his breath drawing her belly tight. "Did you come here for this?"

"No, but I'm all for it." She felt him smile.

She nipped at his lower lip, and he hauled her up his body so that his erection fit between her legs. When she ground herself against him, he groaned. "Don't start this unless you plan to finish it."

"Oh, I'm going to finish it." She touched her mouth to his chest, then to his hard nipples.

She felt the muscles of his stomach clench. His big hands moved up her back, then one slid around her waist to the front of her shorts. His slightly rough fingers slipped inside the waistband. The button gave, then the zipper.

He pushed her shorts and panties to the floor, easing a finger inside her. She made a needy sound deep in her throat; his body went rigid.

Raw, savage need flared in his eyes. "What is this, celebration sex?"

"Call it whatever you want. Just give it to me."

He laughed, giving her a kiss that quickly turned from teasing to deep and demanding. And she surrendered.

Growling impatiently, he picked her up and covered the three steps to the dining table, hooking a foot around the leg of one chair and pulling it to him.

"Wait." Robin stopped him before he could sit.

Sliding a hand into his back pocket, she took out his wallet, then a condom.

"Good thinking," he said roughly.

She opened his shorts, got rid of them and his boxers at the same time.

She curled her hand around him, stroked hard.

He swore. Sitting down, he pulled her between his

legs. His large hands spanned her naked hips as he teasingly stroked the crease of her thighs.

Her legs almost gave out. A muscle in her belly quivered as she realized the searing need inside her could easily rage out of control. He spread open her thin cotton blouse and she watched his hands drag slowly up her rib cage to the lace covering her breasts.

He put his mouth on her, suckling hard, until her nipples strained against the silk of her bra. Overwhelmed with sensation, she gave herself to the dark, seductive draw of his kisses.

His sure touch, the wet fire of his mouth, sent a spear of pure, blinding lust through her. She was barely aware of him ripping open the condom and putting it on.

She shifted impatiently. He pushed off her shirt, nudged down the fabric of her bra and closed his mouth over her.

She inhaled sharply and straddled him, holding his gaze as she sank down on him. His eyes were dark blue, his features tight with restraint. There was a mix of tenderness and hunger on his face that nicked some emotion buried deep inside her.

His gaze moved over her face, then lower, making her skin sizzle as if he were touching her all over. He reached around and unhooked her bra, dropping it to the floor. The possessiveness in his face, the proprietary way he held her, struck at that same raw place inside her and filled her with a sudden urgency.

Why was this happening? She wasn't interested in dissecting her emotions. She wanted *him*. And she wanted him now.

When she shifted to take him deeper, he stopped her, his big hands gripping her hips.

"Just sit here for a minute," he murmured against the

curve of her breast, his mouth damp and warm against her flesh.

A low, hoarse sound escaped her. "I need to move."

"Not yet. I want to feel you."

His skin was dark bronze next to her golden tan. With a rapt look on his face, he studied every inch of her, and she was swept under by a huge, scary wave of emotion.

Her chest tight, she focused on the supple feel of his skin against hers, the soft glide of his lips across the plane of her chest, up her neck to her ear. The faint scent of musk and man mingled with her own scent.

He buried his hands in her hair and kissed her. Slow, deep, hot. Some emotion snaked through her, too quick to define before it was gone.

He pressed a damp kiss on her shoulder, giving her a little shiver. No one had ever been so thorough with her. He touched her like she mattered, as though she were the only thing that did. There was something different about him tonight. It was as if he wanted nothing for himself, wanted only to give to her.

The realization had her going still inside.

Her body was vibrating for his, reaching for the ultimate satisfaction. "Nate," she pleaded in a half whisper. "Please."

He tilted her hips so he could get even deeper inside, just the way he was getting inside her heart. Then they began to move together and she became completely focused on the demands of her body. The barely con-strained frenzy in her blood, the throbbing ache low in her belly.

Maybe it was because he had made her wait, but she needed him at this moment in a way she had never needed another man. Staring into his blue eyes, she realized, in a flash of clarity, he needed her, too.

A huge, searing emotion unfurled in her chest. She was no longer aware of her surroundings, only the big man whose gaze burned right through her, who read her body as though it were his own.

There was no thought in her mind except him. No touch except his. They went over the edge together.

Long minutes later, after their pulses slowed, Nate carried her into his bedroom. They fell into his bed and he pulled her back against him with one arm around her middle.

"Stay," he ordered huskily.

"Okay."

He promptly fell asleep, but Robin didn't.

A thin strip of moonlight was visible beneath his blinds. She lay awake, eyes focused absently on the shadows wavering on the ceiling, across the television at the foot of the bed.

Panic fluttered and she tried to figure out why. What she had shared with Nate was some of the best sex she'd ever had. Shattering enough that her rarely threatened control had jumped the neatly ordered rails of her life.

The thought cut her breath for a second, and that's when she realized what she'd done. She'd fallen for him.

Hard.

All the way.

Chapter 11

The next morning, Robin left Nate's before he woke. She had finally fallen asleep, but in the light of day felt just as unsettled as she had the night before. She jotted him a note telling him she wanted to change clothes before work, though that didn't explain the restlessness she felt, the need to ground herself.

She didn't understand it. The previous evening with Nate had been good. Very, *very* good. So why did she feel so volatile? As though one small thing could make her explode.

Her anxiety could have been due to waiting on the results of the Roper DNA test, but Robin knew that wasn't the case.

It was Nate, she admitted. Or rather the lack of control she felt whenever they were together. At first, the sex had made it easy to ignore anything deeper, but last night had changed that. Had changed everything.

The tenderness in his touch had stripped away any pretense of their relationship being strictly physical. The connection she felt to him was stronger, more intense, more solid than any she'd felt with another person. She had never meant to get this close to him, never wanted to. But she had, proven by the fact that she had gone straight to Nate after talking to her sister.

She had automatically turned to him rather than to Meredith or Terra, the two best friends who had supported her through all the heartache she'd suffered because of her ex and her sister.

Nate had supported her, too. Listened. Then they had gotten naked.

She had known what she was doing, had wanted to do it, but from the moment his lips touched hers she had been helpless to resist. It was as though she had no control over her own body.

In his kitchen last night, with him buried inside her, her carefully managed life had careened off course in a big way. The last time she had experienced this helpless, out-of-control feeling, her wedding imploded and her entire world collapsed. The thought of that happening again had Robin's gut knotting. She had to get back on track right now.

As she walked into the police department, she checked her gun and clip-on holster for the third time, made sure her badge was fastened securely to the waistband of her khaki slacks. Work was just what she needed in order to calm her jittery nerves.

She stashed her purse in the bottom drawer of her desk and headed across the room for coffee. She passed Captain Hager's office on her way to the metal table holding a coffeemaker, foam cups, stir sticks and sugar packets.

On her return, he stopped her. "Daly."

Sipping the hot brew that smelled considerably better than it tasted, she walked into his office. "Sir?"

The wiry, balding man searched through a stack of papers on his desk. "A federally funded position with the FBI has opened up."

Did this affect her? "What kind of position?"

"With their arson investigators to work cold case arson-murders." He paused for a moment to look at her. "It's temporary, and you'd work with them for the term of the grant, a year."

She would? "Sir?"

"With the experience you have you'd be good at something like that."

Unease tickled a spot low on her back, just like it did when her instincts said something was wrong. "Thank you."

"Houston thinks so, too."

Robin froze, her breath jamming under her ribs. "You talked to Houston about this?"

"Actually, he's the one who brought it to me." Dark eyes flickered to her. "He said an assignment like this would be a real coup."

It would. And when had Nate discussed this with her captain? Why hadn't he talked to her about it first? This involved *her. Her job.*

"You would have to move to D.C."

"Move?" Her life was exactly the way she wanted, what she had worked hard to build.

This job, this move would screw up all of that. Panic churned in her gut like acid.

Feeling cornered, Robin listened with half an ear as Hager outlined more details, including when the job would begin.

Nate had some nerve, going behind her back! Turning her life upside down again. Ice-cold shock gave way to burning fury.

She was surprised steam wasn't rising off her skin. She realized Hager was talking to her.

"Once you've had a chance to find out more about it," he said, "let me have your thoughts."

"Sure." Her voice sounded distant; she barely registered answering him. Cold sweat peppered her skin. She had friends and family here. She'd thought she had something with Nate, too. But here he was, working in the background to upend her life. Just like before. He wouldn't get away with this again.

Captain Hager gestured toward her desk, visible through his open blinds. Houston stood with his back to her, talking to Detectives Jack Spencer and Clay Jessup.

"If you have questions," her boss said, "Nate has more information. A Fed buddy of his gave him a heads-up about the position."

"What if I say no? What does that do to my career here?"

Hager leaned back in his chair, gave her a speculative look. "Nothing, I guess. But a chance like this doesn't come around often. You'd get a foot in the door with the Feds, make law enforcement contacts you could use your entire career. Plus, this type of assignment could put you on the fast-track for promotions."

Great, she thought. If she declined, Hager would view her as a deadbeat. A cop who wasn't interested in advancement. Not promotion material.

The more her boss talked, the tighter her chest got. Bowled over by panic and uncertainty, Robin felt suffocated. She murmured agreement and walked out of his office. A red mist hazed her vision as she neared her desk.

Spencer and Jessup, both facing her, lifted a hand in greeting.

"Hi, guys." Her face felt tight, brittle. When Nate turned, she couldn't look at him. If she did, she wouldn't be able to keep from losing her temper. "Houston, could I talk to you for a minute?"

"Sure," he said easily. As though he had no idea what he had done.

As Jack and Clay continued their conversation, Robin walked briskly out of the squad room and down the hall to the stairwell. Her mental circuits were blown. There was no thought, only molten, boiling rage. Behind her, the heavy door squeezed shut.

She caught a faint whiff of Nate's spicy masculine scent and it magnified her anger. Her hand closed over the butt of her gun as she fought to rein in her temper.

"Hey," he said softly. "Why didn't you wake me up before you left this morning?"

"I put a note on the pillow," she gritted out, her control wire thin.

"Yeah, I got it. I just thought—" He broke off when she turned to face him. "What's going on?"

When she didn't answer, he took a step toward her.

She backed away, still reeling from her conversation with Captain Hager.

He went still. "What's happened?"

"What do you think you're doing, talking to my boss about my job? I *have* a job."

Nate's eyes narrowed, his face wary, as if he were tiptoeing through a minefield. "I know."

"And yet you talked to Hager about getting me transferred."

"That's not—"

"Could you not have talked to me first? Bounced the idea off of me?"

"Robin—"

"What gives you the right to try and get me transferred to another assignment? Who the hell do you think you are?"

His shoulders went rigid. "Hold on."

She saw the confusion on his face, but she was too angry to let it stop her. "I don't need you to get me a job. I sure as hell don't need you talking to my boss about a job. Once again, you're sticking your nose in my business!"

The hurt that flared in his eyes had her chest going tight, but she kept going. "You never even mentioned the idea of this FBI position to me. Just because we're sleeping together doesn't mean you can interfere in my life like you did five years ago."

"You're a piece of work, Daly. Do you trust *anyone?*" His eyes glittered dangerously; a muscle in his jaw flexed. "Think about it. Why would I care anything about your job, other than when you have to work with me?"

She drew back, shocked at the savagery in his voice.

"What do you think? That I spoke to Hager because I think you're the only detective in Oklahoma who could handle this position? Get over yourself."

She flushed. Well, when he put it that way, she sounded arrogant, presumptuous. "Okay, maybe I jumped to conclusions."

"*Maybe* you jumped to conclusions? Are you kidding me? For your information," he said coldly, "I had a conversation with your boss. Not a meeting. Not a request for a transfer. You're accusing me of going behind your back in order to get you to do something I supposedly want."

She angled her chin at him, her heart hammering hard. She pushed away a sudden pulse of dread. "Well, then why did you do it?"

"Not to screw up your life, that's for sure." Nate stepped closer, his eyes hard, his words soft and razor-edged. "I derailed your wedding for a good reason. For *you*. And up until now, you agreed I did the right thing. You're the one with the control issue here, not me. I did not go behind your back and I did not ask to get you transferred."

"So you're saying you didn't talk to my captain?" She poked a finger in his chest.

"No, I'm not saying that." He grabbed her wrist, keeping her from touching him again. He towered over her, intimidating and dark. "I asked Hager's opinion on whether you would like that kind of assignment, period."

"And you didn't request he transfer me?"

"No," he said flatly.

The anger and panic leached right out of her. She could feel the blood drain from her face.

Robin thought back over her conversation with the captain. He had said "you" repeatedly. Evidently, he'd meant that in a general sense, not her specifically. Her gut knotted. "The captain—I thought it was a done deal," she said stiffly.

"Well, it wasn't," Nate snapped. "I can't believe you think I would do something like that, especially without talking to you first."

Turning away, he swore, his big hand rubbing his neck. Dread settled over her like a fog.

"I'm sorry I jumped to the wrong conclusion." She'd done more than that. She'd hurt him.

He faced her, white lines of anger etched around his mouth and eyes. His features were stone cold. "Do you know one damn thing about me?"

"I—yes."

"I thought you had moved past what had happened at your wedding, the fact that I *interfered,* but you haven't."

"Yes, I have." Hadn't she? "I know you had my best interest at heart. I know your stepping in was for me."

He slashed a hand through the air. "I've been down this road before. You don't trust me. You may never trust me. I thought we had something good going on here. Obviously, I was wrong."

Panic flooded her like a cold, dark river. "What are you saying? Things are over?"

"Let's put it this way. There isn't much hope for a relationship where one party doesn't trust the other. You don't trust me, that's for sure. If you ever decide you can, give me a call."

Something dark and smoky wound through her, but Robin couldn't define it. And she was too angry to try. Jerking open the door, she walked away.

He didn't stop her.

Two hours later, Nate hadn't stopped fuming. He was back in the fire marshal's office, updating Tom Burke about the investigation. Nate understood why Robin had gotten the wrong impression after talking to her boss, but she hadn't even asked him if it was true. Just jumped down his throat. What he really didn't get was how she could believe he would go behind her back for any reason. Like Kyle had. Like Wendy.

In that stairwell, she had looked at him with the same contempt she had five years earlier. Unbelievable. He was a damn idiot. He had thought he'd gotten past her defenses, gotten to know the real her. That she had gotten to know the real him. It had to be the sex. It was phenomenal. It had never been that way for him with any other woman. That was why he had thought he and Robin had something when they really didn't.

His temple throbbed. And until this investigation wrapped up, he had to work with her.

As Nate explained to his boss about the shaving kit they had found at Joel Roper's former residence, his cell phone rang. A glance down showed Robin's name on the screen. He was sorely tempted to let it go to voice mail, but she could only be calling him about the case.

Excusing himself from his boss, he answered. "Yeah."

"I just got a call from the OSBI lab." Stripped of emotion, her words were a no-nonsense lash of sound.

Nate straightened in his chair. It was probably killing her that she had to call him. If she could've gotten Collier to do it, she probably would have. But their friend was bringing his wife home from the hospital today, so he wasn't working.

"I'm here with Marshal Burke. I'm going to put you on speaker so he can hear this, too."

Once he did that, Robin continued. "The lab matched the DNA from Roper's razor and toothbrush to the cigarette butts we collected at the campground fire."

"Excellent. Do you think his motive for those murders was jealousy?"

"And maybe something else."

Finally getting the evidence they needed to prove Roper was the Mailman filled Nate with satisfaction.

There were only a few loose ends to tie up, then he and Robin could go their separate ways.

Instead of being relieved, the thought annoyed him. "So, we can arrest him and bring him in for questioning."

"Yeah, about that."

Tension lashed Nate's shoulders.

"I called the rig to tell his boss we were coming back down to take him into custody. Roper isn't there. No one knows where he is, but before he went AWOL, his boss overheard him threaten his wife."

"Damn." Nate got to his feet, glancing at his boss. "Our visit tipped him off that we were closing in."

"I think so, too," Robin said.

"He's probably gone after Pattie."

"And we need to get to her first."

We. They. Together. Right. "I'll head for her office."

"I'll meet you there. On my way, I'll call Pattie and let her know what's going on. If she happens to be at home rather than work, I'll call you."

He disconnected.

"Do you need anything from me or this office?" Burke asked.

Nate shook his head. "I'll call OCPD for backup on my way to Mrs. Roper's office."

"Keep me posted."

He nodded, already heading out the door. If Roper did show up at his ex's work place, more people than she would be in danger.

Despite having finally found evidence to prove Joel Roper's guilt, Nate's enthusiasm as he drove to downtown Oklahoma City was outweighed by ambivalence. After the way he and Robin had left things, he doubted she was any more eager to see him than he was to see her.

It didn't matter. He needed to turn off any emotion about her and narrow his focus to the investigation only.

Robin would do the same. She was a professional. She would work with whomever she had to in order to close a case, even Kyle, if necessary. That thought had Nate's jaw clamping hard. The jealous heat that moved through his chest was something he had never felt over another woman. He sure as hell didn't like that, either.

From its mount on the dashboard, his cell phone rang again. Seeing Robin's name on the screen gave him a little jolt as he answered on speaker. Something had happened, or she wouldn't be calling him again so soon.

"Daly?"

"Before I could call Pattie, she called me."

The same apprehension Nate felt was in Robin's voice.

"She's at her office building. She alerted security, but before they made it to her floor, Joel grabbed her outside the restroom. The phone went dead so I didn't get anything else."

"They could be anywhere."

"Right."

"Let's check the office building first and see if we can find them."

"Okay, I'll meet you there."

"See you in a few minutes."

Nate arrived first, going straight to the underground parking garage. He parked near the garage elevator and strode up the ramp to the outdoor lot.

Several black-and-white cruisers arrived; Robin's dark

sedan drove in behind them. He met her halfway to the building's front entrance, trying to shift his gaze from the graceful sway of her hips. *Damn it, stop looking at her.*

The tight set of her mouth told Nate she was irritated. At seeing him? "I've seen no sign of her."

"Neither have I."

"Shoot." Concern streaked across Robin's features. "I'll have some uniforms go up to her office, station some on the above-ground parking lot, too. You and I can search the stairwells."

"I'll take an elevator to the top floor and start down."

"I'll begin at the bottom."

Nate nodded, opening the door for her and following her inside. He was glad he wouldn't have to work shoulder to shoulder with her. He might still be angry, but that didn't mean he wanted her any less.

He stopped at the service elevator, where the building's security manager handed him the key. He expected Robin to walk past him to the other side of the building and the entrance to the stairwell.

Instead, she paused, her gaze sliding over him. All his muscles pulled tight. What was she looking at?

"Good, you have your gun."

"Yes." He touched the weapon tucked into the waistband of his jeans.

"Let's use radios instead of our cell phones." She handed him a radio like the one she held. "I don't want to take the chance we might lose touch."

Nate nodded, climbing into the elevator. As the doors closed, he heard her request that all available officers begin searching floor by floor.

Once he reached the thirtieth floor, he started back

down via the stairs. He radioed his location to Robin, keeping her posted on his progress as he reached each floor.

She did the same.

Nate was breathing hard by the time he reached floor twenty. Robin was panting, too, when she checked in on floor eight. The sound of her exertion made him think about when she had been breathing hard the night before, for a whole different reason.

He rounded the end of one flight, rushed down the next one. And saw something in the corner behind the exit door. As he reached it, he identified a woman's shoe and a cell phone. He shared the find with Robin.

"Is the phone Pattie's?"

He pressed redial and Robin's number popped up on the screen. "Yes. You're the last person she talked to."

"So Joel didn't use the elevator. He came up the stairs."

"And probably grabbed her."

"Keep checking. I want to make sure they aren't in any of the stairwells."

Nate pocketed Pattie's cell phone and continued down the stairs. There was still no sign of the Ropers when he reached the landing on floor fourteen, and he stopped, hearing the muffled rush of footsteps coming toward him.

In a few seconds, Robin came into view. She stopped at the base of the stairs. Disappointment streaked across her face. "No sign of them?"

"No."

"The uniforms have been checking in with me. There's no sign of the Ropers in the garage, the basement or in her office, so Joel has taken her somewhere else."

"They have to be in this building," Nate said. "There's

no access from here to other buildings or parking facilities."

Robin's radio crackled and a male voice said, "Detective, the chopper pilot spotted two people on the roof."

"The roof." She said it with distaste, as though she were talking about a crypt.

They jumped onto the service elevator and rode to the top floor.

Even in the poor light of the enclosed space, Nate could see the waxy cast to her skin. She was worried about her vertigo.

Stepping out of the elevator, they headed for the door that led to the highest point of the building.

Nate glanced at her, seeing no reason why she should go out there if it weren't necessary. "I can check this out quickly, if you want."

The look she gave him could have crushed rock.

"Never mind," he said before she could lay into him. He should've squashed his concern and kept his mouth shut.

Not wanting to spook Joel if he was up there, Nate flipped off his radio as did Robin. Then he followed her through the doorway.

The roof appeared to be an acre wide. The flat concrete surface was broken by two commercial-size air-conditioning units. One was in the far corner and one was just feet away, blocking their view of part of the roof. So far, there was no sign of anyone.

Between the rumble of the machine and the whoosh of passing traffic on the nearby highway, it was difficult to hear, but he was still careful to close the door as quietly as possible.

Ahead of him, Robin peered around the corner of the giant air-conditioning unit. She pulled back and sagged against the wall, closing her eyes. "Yes, it's them."

Chapter 12

Robin ducked inside the building to radio for backup, while Nate stayed outside to keep an eye on things. A woman's scream was barely audible beneath the rumble of the air-conditioning unit.

Robin rushed back outside to Nate, touching his shoulder. When he withdrew the slightest bit, she knew it was because of what she'd said to him earlier. Her heart squeezed tight. "Backup is on the way. I told them to wait for our signal before they come out here. The last thing we need is to spook Joel. We can't wait. We need to get her away from him."

"I've been thinking about that."

"Joel's still at the far edge of the roof, and Pattie's still on the ledge?"

"Yes. He's not armed that I can tell." Nate kept his gaze on the couple.

Robin had to lean in close so she could hear him.

"I think I should approach from the front and work my way to the edge. You can come up behind him."

So Nate was thinking about her vertigo. Was he trying to make things easier on her by keeping her from the edge? Or trying to minimize the chances of her screwing up because of her problem?

When she saw his face she knew. Even after what she had said to him, what she had thought of him, he was trying to protect her. She could tell he expected her to argue with his suggestion, but she wasn't going to.

She was reminded of how he had protected her five years earlier. In a painful flash of clarity, she realized she had made a huge mistake. Not only by accusing him of interfering in her life, but also by accepting his decision to end things between them.

But now wasn't the time to think about that. That was for when the situation with Joel Roper was resolved.

Robin looked up at Nate. "Do you think he plans to start a fire? Try to burn her?"

"I have yet to see anything flammable."

"So he's using the threat of pushing her off the ledge to make her do what he wants?"

"Yes. He's improvising, which means he didn't have time to plan this out very well. Or he didn't take the time."

Robin agreed. She wished Nate would look at her. "Ready?"

Despite his dark sunglasses, she could tell when his gaze met hers. "You sure you're okay to do this?"

"Give me a break."

Irritation flashed across his rugged features. "Don't get your panties in a twist. I just don't want to lose our chance at him. And I don't want anyone to get hurt."

She had no right to feel disappointed that he hadn't

said he didn't want *her* getting hurt, yet she did. Stupid. There was no time for this. She adjusted her sunglasses and moved down the wall toward the back of the air-conditioning unit.

When she was in place, she glanced over her shoulder and signaled Nate. As he drew his weapon and disappeared around the corner, Robin did the same, working her way to the opposite corner. She could see Nate now. Pattie and Joel, too.

When Nate's gaze flickered to her, she gave him a thumbs-up.

Gun leveled, he moved away from the unit and into the open. "Joel, it's Agent Houston."

Holding on to his ex-wife's leg, he jerked toward Nate.

"Stay back!"

Pattie wobbled, screaming as she grabbed Joel's shoulder.

Halting several feet from the pair, Nate kept his voice calm. "Take it easy, Joel. I just want to talk to you, make sure everyone's okay."

Robin crept forward, her weapon trained on the desperate man who was focused on her partner.

Nate shifted his attention to the woman on the ledge.

"Pattie, are you all right?"

"Yes," she sobbed.

Even from here, Robin could tell the woman was trembling. Fear made her eyes wild.

Nate eased closer. "Let her go, Roper."

Joel grabbed Pattie's wrist and yanked hard. "Get back, man! If you don't, I'll push her."

Screeching, she fell forward, catching herself by grabbing on to her ex-husband's arm.

Robin inched along, trying to stay out of Roper's peripheral vision. She was almost directly behind him.

Sirens sounded nearby.

"You better get rid of those cops," Joel ordered.

Nate kept his gun on the man. "You can end this right now, Joel. Let her go."

"No!"

"Tell me what you want." Nate remained still. "Why are you doing this?"

"I want her to pay for taking my kids away from me."

"Is that why you killed and burned those men?"

Keep him talking, Nate, Robin thought, as she snuck up behind the suspect.

"Who said I killed anybody? She took away my kids," Joel informed them bitterly. "Why shouldn't she pay for that?"

Over his head, Pattie caught sight of Robin, and her eyes widened. Shaking her head, Robin cautioned the other woman to stay quiet.

She was close enough now to see tears streaking Pattie's face, running her mascara. She also had a hole in the right knee of her stockings.

Nate shifted from one foot to the other, gradually working his way closer to the edge of the roof.

Joel started, violently enough that Pattie wobbled. Arms flailing, she clutched at his shoulder. "Joel!" she screamed. "Let me go!"

"Shut up!" Roaring, he lunged at his ex and shoved her. Pattie cried out, toppling backward.

Nate and Robin both dove for the woman. Robin slammed into the ledge hard enough to knock the wind out of her, catching Pattie's wrist as she went over the side. Joel threw himself into Nate and both men went down.

Behind her, Robin heard grunts, the sound of fists hitting flesh. Pattie's suspended weight nearly yanked Robin's arm out of its socket. Clamping both hands around the woman's bony wrist, she braced her knees against the ledge.

Pattie twisted frantically over the side of the building.

Muscles burning, joints strained, Robin yelled, "Be still or I won't be able to pull you up on my own."

She also wouldn't be able to hang on, but she didn't say that. "Can you get a foothold anywhere?"

"No."

"Okay." Keeping her gaze locked on her feet, Robin pulled. "Here you go."

The tendons in her arms felt as though they might snap. Struggling, breathing hard, Robin finally managed to wrangle the woman up about four inches. Then her arm slid in Robin's grip.

Her ears ringing from Pattie's screams, Robin dug her heels into the roof's surface, cold fear slicing through her. She wasn't sure how much longer she could hold on. Behind her, Nate and Roper were still fighting.

"Help! Help!" Pattie screamed.

"Stop panicking!" Robin snapped. Acting on instinct to try and calm the woman, Robin peered over the edge, locking gazes with her. "Pattie, look at me! Don't take your eyes off me."

The redhead obeyed.

Robin had hoped that by not looking down, she could escape her vertigo, but the ground began to tilt. Spots danced in front of her eyes.

Pattie's nails dug into Robin's flesh, but even the

bite of pain couldn't help her stave off the dizziness. She heard the sliding snap of Nate's gun, the rush of footsteps announcing the arrival of backup.

Sky, buildings, concrete spiraled into one giant funnel. Cold sweat broke out over her body. Blackness closed in from the edges of her vision, but she was helpless against it. She could feel her control slipping away. Panic was the last thing she registered before she fell flat on her back, her head banging the concrete.

Warm heavy hands cupped her shoulders. "Daly?"

Nate. She opened her eyes, his features blurry as the world continued to spin. "Pattie?" she asked.

"She's fine." What was that emotion in his eyes? Concern? Anger? "You managed to hold on to her until I got Joel cuffed."

"Thank goodness. Can you help me sit up?"

He did, releasing her when she managed to stay upright.

"What about Joel?"

"He's waiting for us to question him." Nate helped her stand and they walked over to where the suspect waited, rage still burning in his eyes.

Nate studied the man. "Joel, we matched your DNA to some cigarette butts we found at the Spur Creek campground fire. We know you set that blaze and killed Hal Trahan as well as four other people in different fires. You're the arsonist we've been looking for."

"You don't have my DNA," he glowered.

"We do. We got it from a razor and toothbrush you left at your old house."

Robin's pulse steadied. "Roper, you're going away for a long time. Be glad you didn't add your children's mother to the list of people you murdered."

"I wish I had. Why should she be allowed to take my family away?"

"Because you're a psycho, Joel!" the woman accused shrilly.

"Pattie," Robin warned.

Joel snarled at his ex.

"Roper," Nate said sharply. "Why did you kill and burn those men?"

"Because Pattie slept with them."

"I didn't sleep with Hal," she denied.

"You would have."

"He was just a friend!"

"So, you were jealous?" Robin asked Joel.

"No. I did it so I could get my kids away from this slut."

"What about the woman you killed? What did Sheila Bane ever do to you?"

"I never meant to kill her." Joel raised his cuffed wrists and dragged a forearm across his perspiring forehead. "Just her husband, who was having an affair with Pattie."

Nate nodded. "So you spent your days off following her, then planting accelerant at the victims' residences the night before you were due back at the rig?"

Pattie stared in horrified disbelief at her ex-husband. "You freak!" she shrieked. "Our kids shouldn't be around you at all!"

"Get him out of here," Robin said to the waiting police officers.

She drew in a deep breath, sliding a look at Nate. "We did it. We caught the Mailman."

"Yeah." He sounded relieved, but also guarded. Distant.

Because of her, she realized. Because of what had happened between them earlier.

"This paramedic is going to check you out," he said. "Make sure you're okay."

She nodded as he moved away, flipping open his cell phone and asking for Marshal Burke. He explained to his boss what had happened with the Ropers.

"Detective?" A young female paramedic checked Robin's vitals. "Are you still dizzy?"

"No, I'm fine now."

"Okay." With a smile, the paramedic moved away.

Several feet away, Nate now stood talking to Pattie Roper. A couple of times, he glanced over at Robin. She could read nothing on his face or in the eyes hidden behind his sunglasses.

She wanted to thank him for helping her. He probably would have preferred pushing her over the ledge, she thought wryly.

She watched as Pattie Roper walked over to her.

"You saved my life." The woman's voice shook. "Thank you."

"You're welcome." Instead of being irritated over getting knocked on her dizzy butt, Robin was grateful that Nate had been there to help her. "I suspect you owe more thanks to Agent Houston than me."

"That's what he said about you." Pattie gave a teary smile.

Warmth spread through Robin. "Oh."

He had saved both of them. *Not bad for a day's work,* she thought. After hugging her, the other woman left with the waiting paramedics.

Robin's cell phone vibrated and she pulled it from the pocket of her slacks. It was her captain. As she reassured him she was fine and that the Mailman had been apprehended, her gaze slowly scanned the roof for Nate.

She didn't see him anywhere among the growing number of law enforcement personnel.

Flipping her phone shut, she walked to the air-conditioning unit where they had started. He wasn't there, either. He was gone. Without a word.

There was a hollowness in her chest. Deep, sharp. How could he have just left?

Well, after what she had accused him of, why wouldn't he?

Pushing him away had been a huge mistake. As had not admitting her feelings earlier.

She was in love with him.

For a second, she couldn't breathe. She was in love with Nate Houston.

For five years, she had blamed him for ruining her life. She knew now that he had been protecting her, that he had saved her from marrying a cheat. And despite that, panic had driven her to accuse him earlier.

After her wedding-that-wasn't, she had vowed to control every part of her life. She had done it so well that all she had now was that control. And an aching emptiness.

After wrapping things up at the scene, Robin pulled up at Presley's police department. It was just before noon. With everything that had happened that morning, it seemed as though four days had passed rather than four hours.

When she finished with Roper, she intended to talk to Nate. Well, grovel was more like it.

Just as she started to open her car door, she saw him walk out of the police department. He headed toward his SUV, which sat in the shade beneath a tree at the opposite end of the parking lot. Her gaze moved hungrily over his long-lined athletic frame, from the strong column of his neck, to his hard chest, down his powerful legs. She liked the way he walked, his stride easy and confident.

He would need her reports in order to finish his own paperwork for the task force, but he obviously wasn't going to wait around for them. She considered and dismissed waving him down. She didn't want to start a conversation here. It was too public. Plus business needed to come first.

Nate climbed into his truck and drove away. Her chest squeezed hard. What if she had ruined everything? A paralyzing chill came over her. She couldn't bear the thought that she might have driven him away for good. One thing gave her hope: he hadn't left the crime scene until he had made sure she was okay. She held on to that.

Her interview with Roper went quickly, especially once she learned Nate had gotten a written confession from the guy. Roper wasn't a copycat and hadn't held a grudge against Nate. He'd learned about using chlorine powder and petroleum jelly as an accelerant from an article in the newspaper. What were the odds the guy had decided to use that same method on a case Nate was assigned? Weird.

Two hours after watching Nate walk away, Robin stood on his front porch. She was relieved to see his SUV in the driveway. She hadn't called to make sure he was home. She was afraid he might not answer. Or that if he did answer, he would tell her not to come.

The sweat slicking her palms wasn't caused by the midday heat. She rang the bell and a few seconds later the door opened. He wore the same navy polo shirt with the fire marshal's emblem and navy slacks she had last seen him in. His eyes flared hotly when he saw her, then his face closed against her. Robin could read nothing on his implacable features.

"Did you come to give me copies of your reports?"

"No."

He arched a brow, his body rigid. Waiting.

She couldn't lose him. He had to hear her out, let her explain. "You said if I decided I could trust you, then I should find you. That's why I'm here."

He looked skeptical. "A few hours ago, you were pretty damn sure you didn't trust me. I have trouble accepting that you changed your mind so fast."

They still stood in his doorway, cool air wafting out to mix with humid heat. "I'd like to apologize. And explain."

"That isn't going to change the fact that you actually believed I interfered with your job."

She had hurt him even more than she realized. What if he turned her away? The same sharp hollowness she'd felt when he had left the crime scene bored through her.

"Please."

After a moment he nodded, but rather than invite her inside the house, he stepped out, closing the door behind him.

Robin tried not to read anything into that, like perhaps he was shutting her out of his house *and* his life for good.

"All right." Face guarded, he folded his arms.

Her throat suddenly dry and tight, she licked her lips nervously. "You said I have a control issue and you're right. First, I apologize for ripping into you. Also for jumping to conclusions, instead of asking you about your conversation with my boss. Deep down, I knew you hadn't gone behind my back or messed with my job."

Blowing out a harsh breath, he pinched the bridge of his nose. "Is this where you get to the explaining part? Because I was there and you sure seemed to believe it."

"I was wrong to make you feel that way. I used that as an excuse to push you away. I…panicked."

His gaze lasered into hers as he leaned one shoulder against the door. Despite the tension pulsing between them, he was still listening.

"When Captain Hager told me you had talked to him about a new assignment, I was overwhelmed. I don't know if he made it sound as though it were a done deal or if I just perceived it that way. Regardless, I made assumptions I shouldn't have. After I left this morning, I took a long, hard look at myself."

He said nothing. Robin trembled. He had every right to tell her to get lost. She didn't want to give him the chance.

"What happened with Kyle threw me into a tailspin. The rejection, the emotional chaos affected me more than I would ever have thought possible. The only way I seemed able to move on was to order my life."

"Start controlling things," Nate said.

"Yes, especially my emotions. Then you came along. All of a sudden, I couldn't control anything. Not the past. Not having to work with you, not my vertigo, which just made me feel even more helpless. Then when we got physical, I was completely swept away."

His eyes narrowed. "You can't hold that against me."

"I don't. That isn't what I mean. I'm trying to explain

how I felt. It was as though you were controlling all of me, as though I were being manipulated. The last time I felt that way was at my wedding. It scared me to death, and when we made love last night, I realized I had feelings for you that I haven't ever had for anyone."

"Except Kyle."

"No, *anyone*." She wanted to touch him, but Nate's stance clearly warned her off. "It freaked me out."

"No kidding," he muttered.

She was really screwing this up. "What I said to you this morning was wrong and I'm sorry. I'm afraid I may have ruined everything. The thought of walking away from you terrifies me more than the possibility that things might not work out with us. A bigger mistake than the one I made this morning would be not to come here and ask for another chance. Not to tell you—" Tears blurring her vision, she swallowed around the lump in her throat. "I love you, Nate."

He finally moved, closing the distance between them and nudging her chin up with one knuckle. His blue eyes were tender. "I love you, too," he said softly. "But I'm not sure that's enough to make things work between us."

In an instant, her joy changed to ice-cold fear. "What do you mean? You can't forgive me?"

"There's no need. I understand why you said what you did."

"Then what is it?"

He brushed his thumb along her bottom lip. "It's my turn to explain something to you."

She nodded, going still inside. Refusing to even think that this could be the end for them.

"When you accused me of going behind your back, I remembered all the times Stephanie did that to me.

All the times I trusted her when she was lying. After a while, I didn't trust anything she said, not even the smallest thing, like going to the store."

Raw emotion edged his words; his eyes were troubled. "Sweetheart, if you can't trust me, we have nothing to build on."

Hope bloomed inside her. "If I didn't trust you," she said softly, cupping his jaw, "I wouldn't be baring my soul to you."

"I get why you panicked." He pulled her close. "I never thought I would want to take a chance on a relationship again, either, but I do. With you."

"Me, too." She slid her arms around his neck. "Kiss me."

"I want forever, Robin. I don't want to scare you off, but you need to know that's how things are for me."

"Surprisingly, I'm not spooked." *Awed, yes.*

His arms tightened around her. "You can have time to get used to it, as much time as you want, but I'm not going anywhere. I need to know that you aren't, either. I want to hear you say it."

Robin's heart clenched with a sweet pain as she recognized the same vulnerability, the same naked need on his face that she felt. "I'm not going anywhere."

The panic she would have felt in the past didn't come. She rolled up on her tiptoes and kissed him.

"When you're ready to marry me, you let me know."

Her breath caught. Drawing back to look into his eyes, she waited for the dread she had expected to feel if she ever fell in love again. It wasn't there. Instead, there was a bone-deep certainty that this was right. "Yes, I will."

"You will what? Marry me or let me know?"

"Yes." She tugged his head down to hers, but he stopped before their lips touched. She huffed out an exasperated breath. "Nate."

He grinned. "When you decide to accept my proposal, you better be prepared to go through with it, because I won't make the mistake of leaving you at the altar."

"You could get a lot closer to the altar if you would kiss me now."

So he did, long and slow and deep. As he swung her up in his arms and headed inside his house, she murmured against his lips, "Okay, I'm ready to go through with it."

And two months later, she did.

Epilogue

On a sultry evening in mid-August, Robin stood in the bride's dressing area of a small church. Her gown was a strapless sheath in blush pink, a pale shade of the bridesmaids' deep pink dresses.

It might have been only two months since she and Nate had realized their feelings, but they had shared every part of themselves with each other, good and bad. As a result, Robin was even more sure that she and this man belonged together.

She watched in the full-length mirror as Meredith put the finishing touches on her hair, pulled up on the sides with a thin headband of crystals, leaving her hair to cascade in curls down the back.

Terra fastened the string of pearls belonging to Robin's mom, who was doing a last-minute check with Wendy, to make sure everything was in place. Robin's sister had seemed touched and surprised when Robin had asked her to be a member of the wedding party. Robin was glad Wendy had accepted; it was a big step in their new relationship.

"You look perfect." Terra stood behind her, meeting her gaze in the mirror. Her friend's green eyes were teary.

Meredith stepped inside and closed the door, coming over to hug Robin. "I never thought you'd consider marriage again let alone do it. I'm so glad you did. Are you nervous?"

"Yes, but not because I'm wondering if this is right. It's because I'm excited, if you can believe it."

Her friend smiled. "Everyone has been seated. Kiley's down the hall helping Collier with his best man duties."

Terra fussed with the necklace clasp. "I saw Walker and Jen McClain in the chapel, and also Clay and Shelby."

Terra's cell phone rang. After a brief exchange, she hung up. "That was Jack. He said Nate's SUV is covered in shaving cream and shoe polish. He parked our car on the other side of the building for you guys to use. I'll put the keys in your purse."

"Thanks, both of you." Robin hugged her two friends.

Orchestral sounds of the classical piece she had chosen to begin the wedding floated down the hall. Nate's sister and brother-in-law were also in the wedding party. Becca picked up Robin's bouquet and handed it to her.

After a quick hug, Becca opened the door. Robin's mom and Wendy each kissed her cheek, then the bridal party made their way down the hallway to the building's foyer and chapel.

Her stomach fluttered. This was really going to happen.

At the first notes of the wedding march, she rounded the corner and stopped in the doorway of the chapel. Surprised to see Nate, her eyes widened.

With an arrested stare on his face, he came to her, murmuring, "You look incredible."

"Thanks." Wanting to laugh with joy, she whispered, "What are you doing?"

"Waiting for you. I didn't want you to have to wonder if I was at the altar."

Tears filled her eyes. She had reassured him again and again that she wouldn't have flashbacks to the wedding-that-wasn't. She remembered it, sure, but she now thought of it as a pit stop in the broken road that had brought her and Nate together.

His gesture, so typically thoughtful of her feelings, made her fall even more in love with him.

He took her hand, brushed a kiss across her knuckles. "I have no doubts about marrying you, and I don't want you to have any about me."

"I don't." Her throat tightened. "Not one."

"I want to walk down the aisle with you," he said softly.

Incredibly touched, speechless for a moment, she clutched the hand that still held hers.

"Your dad said he doesn't mind if you don't walk with him."

"Nate Houston, don't you dare make me cry."

He grinned. "So that's a yes?"

She nodded, adding a tremulous, "I love you."

"I love you, too." His eyes smiled into hers. "You ready?"

"Yes."

Lacing her fingers with his, they walked toward their new life together.

* * * * *

*Harlequin offers a romance for every mood!
See below for a sneak peek
from our paranormal romance line,
Silhouette® Nocturne™.
Enjoy a preview of REUNION by USA TODAY
bestselling author Lindsay McKenna.*

Aella closed her eyes and sensed a distinct shift, like movement from the world around her to the unseen world.

She opened her eyes. And had a slight shock at the man standing ten feet away. He wasn't just any man. Her heart leaped and pounded. He reminded her of a fierce warrior from an ancient civilization. Incan? She wasn't sure but she felt his deep power and masculinity.

I'm Aella. Are you the guardian of this sacred site? she asked, hoping her telepathy was strong.

Fox's entire body soared with joy. Fox struggled to put his personal pleasure aside.

Greetings, Aella. I'm the assistant guardian to this sacred area. You may call me Fox. How can I be of service to you, Aella? he asked.

I'm searching for a green sphere. A legend says that the Emperor Pachacuti had seven emerald spheres created for the Emerald Key necklace. He had seven of his priestesses and priests travel the world to hide these spheres from evil forces. It is said that when all seven spheres are found, restrung and worn, that Light will return to the Earth. The fourth sphere is here, at your sacred site. Are you aware of it? Aella held her breath. She loved looking at him, especially his sensual mouth. The desire to kiss him came out of nowhere.

Fox was stunned by the request. *I know of the*

Emerald Key necklace because I served the emperor at the time it was created. However, I did not realize that one of the spheres is here.

Aella felt sad. Why? Every time she looked at Fox, her heart felt as if it would tear out of her chest. *May I stay in touch with you as I work with this site?* she asked.

Of course. Fox wanted nothing more than to be here with her. To absorb her ephemeral beauty and hear her speak once more.

Aella's spirit lifted. What *was* this strange connection between them? Her curiosity was strong, but she had more pressing matters. In the next few days, Aella knew her life would change forever. How, she had no idea....

Look for REUNION
by USA TODAY bestselling author
Lindsay McKenna,
available April 2010, only from
Silhouette® Nocturne™.

Copyright © 2009 by Lindsay McKenna

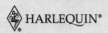
HARLEQUIN®

INTRIGUE®

WILL THIS REUNITED FAMILY
BE STRONG ENOUGH TO EXPOSE
A LURKING KILLER?

FIND OUT IN THIS ALL-NEW
THRILLING TRILOGY FROM TOP
HARLEQUIN INTRIGUE AUTHOR

B.J. DANIELS

WHITEHORSE
MONTANA

Winchester Ranch

GUN-SHY BRIDE—*April 2010*

HITCHED—*May 2010*

TWELVE-GAUGE GUARDIAN—
June 2010

www.eHarlequin.com

HI69465

Stay up-to-date on all your romance-reading news with the brand-new Harlequin *Inside Romance!*

The Harlequin *Inside Romance* is a **FREE** quarterly newsletter highlighting our upcoming series releases and promotions!

Click on the *Inside Romance* link on the front page of www.eHarlequin.com or e-mail us at InsideRomance@Harlequin.ca to sign up to receive your FREE newsletter today!

You can also subscribe by writing to us at: HARLEQUIN BOOKS
Attention: Customer Service Department
P.O. Box 9057, Buffalo, NY 14269-9057

Please allow 4-6 weeks for delivery of the first issue by mail.

IRNBPAQ309

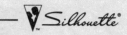

SPECIAL EDITION

**INTRODUCING A BRAND-NEW MINISERIES
FROM *USA TODAY* BESTSELLING AUTHOR**

KASEY MICHAELS

SECOND-CHANCE BRIDAL

At twenty-eight, widowed single mother
Elizabeth Carstairs thinks she's left love behind
forever....until she meets Will Hollingsbrook.
Her sons' new baseball coach is the handsomest
man she's ever seen—and the more time they
spend together, the more undeniable the
connection between them. But can Elizabeth
leave the past behind and open her heart to
a second chance at love?

FIND OUT IN

SUDDENLY A BRIDE

*Available in April
wherever books are sold.*

Visit Silhouette Books at www.eHarlequin.com

SSE65517

HARLEQUIN® Romance®

ROMANCE, RIVALRY
AND A FAMILY REUNITED

THE BRIDES
of
BELLA ROSA

William Valentine and his beloved wife, Lucia, live
a beautiful life together, but when his former love Rosa
and the secret family they had together resurface,
an instant rivalry is formed. Can these families
get through the past and come together as one?

Step into the world of Bella Rosa
beginning this April with

Beauty and the Reclusive Prince
by
RAYE MORGAN

Eight volumes to collect and treasure!

www.eHarlequin.com

HRI7650

Silhouette Desire

OLIVIA GATES

BILLIONAIRE, M.D.

Dr. Rodrigo Valderrama has it all…
everything but the woman he's secretly
desired and despised. A woman forbidden
to him—his brother's widow.
And she's pregnant.

Cybele was injured in a plane crash
and lost her memory. All she knows is
she's falling for the doctor who has swept her
away to his estate to heal. If only the secrets
in his eyes didn't promise to tear
them forever apart.

Available March wherever you buy books.

Always Powerful, Passionate and Provocative.

Visit Silhouette Books at www.eHarlequin.com

SD73018

Single father Ian Ferguson's daughter is finally coming out of her shell thanks to the twenty-three-year-old tutor Alexa Michaels. Although Alexa is young—and too pretty—she graduated from the school of hard knocks and is challenging some of Ian's old-school ways. Could this dad learn some valuable lessons about love, family and faith from the least likely teacher?

Look for

Love Lessons

by

Margaret Daley

Helping Hands Homeschooling

*Available April
wherever books are sold.*

Steeple
Hill®

LI87590

www.SteepleHill.com

HARLEQUIN
Ambassadors

Want to share your passion for reading Harlequin® Books?

Become a Harlequin Ambassador!

Harlequin Ambassadors are a group of passionate and well-connected readers who are willing to share their joy of reading Harlequin® books with family and friends.

You'll be sent all the tools you need to spark great conversation, including free books!

All we ask is that you share the romance with your friends and family!

You'll also be invited to have a say in new book ideas and exchange opinions with women just like you!

To see if you qualify* to be a Harlequin Ambassador, please visit www.HarlequinAmbassadors.com.

*Please note that not everyone who applies to be a Harlequin Ambassador will qualify. For more information please visit www.HarlequinAmbassadors.com.

Thank you for your participation.

BAPO9BPA

REQUEST YOUR FREE BOOKS!

2 FREE NOVELS
PLUS
2 FREE GIFTS!

ROMANTIC SUSPENSE

Sparked by Danger, Fueled by Passion.

YES! Please send me 2 FREE Silhouette® Romantic Suspense novels and my 2 FREE gifts (gifts are worth about $10). After receiving them, if I don't wish to receive any more books, I can return the shipping statement marked "cancel." If I don't cancel, I will receive 4 brand-new novels every month and be billed just $4.24 per book in the U.S. or $4.99 per book in Canada. That's a saving of 15% off the cover price! It's quite a bargain! Shipping and handling is just 50¢ per book in the U.S. and 75¢ per book in Canada.* I understand that accepting the 2 free books and gifts places me under no obligation to buy anything. I can always return a shipment and cancel at any time. Even if I never buy another book from Silhouette, the two free books and gifts are mine to keep forever.

240 SDN E39A 340 SDN E39M

Name	(PLEASE PRINT)	
Address		Apt. #
City	State/Prov.	Zip/Postal Code

Signature (if under 18, a parent or guardian must sign)

Mail to the **Silhouette Reader Service:**

IN U.S.A.: P.O. Box 1867, Buffalo, NY 14240-1867
IN CANADA: P.O. Box 609, Fort Erie, Ontario L2A 5X3

Not valid for current subscribers to Silhouette Romantic Suspense books.

Want to try two free books from another line?
Call 1-800-873-8635 or visit www.morefreebooks.com.

* Terms and prices subject to change without notice. Prices do not include applicable taxes. N.Y. residents add applicable sales tax. Canadian residents will be charged applicable provincial taxes and GST. Offer not valid in Quebec. This offer is limited to one order per household. All orders subject to approval. Credit or debit balances in a customer's account(s) may be offset by any other outstanding balance owed by or to the customer. Please allow 4 to 6 weeks for delivery. Offer available while quantities last.

Your Privacy: Silhouette is committed to protecting your privacy. Our Privacy Policy is available online at www.eHarlequin.com or upon request from the Reader Service. From time to time we make our lists of customers available to reputable third parties who may have a product or service of interest to you. If you would prefer we not share your name and address, please check here. ☐

Help us get it right—We strive for accurate, respectful and relevant communications. To clarify or modify your communication preferences, visit us at www.ReaderService.com/consumerschoice.